Lidija Dimkovska
Grandma Non-Oui

This book was first published
in Macedonian as No-Ui, 2016

Text © Lidija Dimkovska, 2024
Translation © Christina E. Kramer

The right of Lidija DImkovska, to be
identified as the author of this work has
been asserted in accordance with the
Copyright, Designs and Patents Act, 1988

First published in 2024 by Istros Books
London, United Kingdom
www.istrosbooks.com

Design and layout: pikavejica.com

Printed by CMP, Poole, Dorset, UK

ISBN: 978-1-912545-40-7

**NATIONAL
ENDOWMENT
for the ARTS**
arts.gov

This project is supported in part by the
National Endowment for the Arts.

ARTS COUNCIL
ENGLAND

Supported using public funding by

**ARTS COUNCIL
ENGLAND**

Lidija Dimkovska

Grandma Non-Oui

translated by
Christina E. Kramer

istrosbooks

All characters and events are fictional, except historical ones

'You exist when someone thinks of you.'

Princesses,
FERNANDO LEON DE ARANOA

NONNA, yesterday Papà told me about a group of tourists speaking a Slavic language that boarded the minibus he was driving back from Scopello. There were several women and men and five or six children. Papà asked them what language they were speaking, and they told him it was Slovenian. They had come to Castellammare for a one-week trip, and they were enchanted by Scopello. You remember, we went there once, too; just think, only once, by car, before Papà started driving the Russo minibuses. Isn't it strange? The people who come to Sicily as tourists simply must visit Scopello, but those of us who live here go once in our lives and that's it. Take Papà, for example. He drives a minibus but he never goes anywhere himself.

You know, I read an interesting statistic a while ago in *La Republica*: the residents of a city, or even of a whole country, rarely visit their local museums unless they're taken there on a school trip, and that is, in fact, the point of school trips: to give the people who live in a city or a country the chance to visit their own national landmarks at least while they're in school, because once they finish, it never occurs to them to visit the museums they pass every day as they hurry about their daily routines. The journalist who conducted the survey even provided some specific examples: a fifty-year old woman in Florence had been working for twenty-five years in a law office near the Florence Cathedral Santa Maria dei Fiori, and even though she passed the cathedral every day on her way to and from work, even though she had smoked in front of the building for years, her eyes staring directly at the cathedral, she had never actually gone inside, and whenever she thought about going in, there were too many tourists at the entrance, so she'd say to herself, 'Ok, maybe next time.' And that's how her life continues. The journalist cited similar examples from Paris, London, Madrid, as well as in smaller places with famous landmarks; it's nearly the same everywhere. I thought about this because Papà said the Slovenian tourists didn't go just once to Scopello, immediately the day after they arrived in Castellammare del Golfo, but they liked it so much they went again yesterday before leaving Sicily, this time on an outing organized by the snorkeling centre and they explored the rocks that jut up from the water and are so famous that people knew about Scopello even in Slovenia. Twice to Scopello in seven days! Papà was on the minibus shift yesterday when they were returning from their second visit, enchanted once again by the buildings, and even more so by the view of the sea and the rocks. Imagine this: he told them he understood a few words in their language, and in a mixture of English and Croatian he told them that his mother, you, was from Split, from Spalato; they were surprised and they smiled, repeating the word Split, yes, Split, Croatia, Yugoslavia. As he drove them to Castellammare del Golfo, he told them about you and our family, and about me as well, talking the whole time in a mix of English and Italian with an occasional Croatian word thrown in. He told them my name was Nedjeljka, the same as yours, and that I knew Croatian, the only one in the whole family, and they wondered what my name sounded like in Sicilian, and Papà said, 'We all call her Neda, just like we called her Grandma Neda, but all her official documents say Nedjeljka.' They understood that you came to Castellammare del Golfo in 1947 because of Granddad, and that at that time the Mafia ruled the city, which Papà explained by repeating 'boom, boom, boom' several times. 'So, what's it like now?' one of them asked. 'Now, life is peaceful, beautiful,' he said. 'There's no more Mafia.' And then he went back to talking about you, how it was hard for you here as a foreigner, and how you visited Split only two times, and when you were about to go for what would have been the third time, you left the airplane ticket in the drawer because Granddad had died. He even told them that. I imagine that he was excited meeting them and he spoke quickly so he could tell them all the things he wouldn't say a word about to anyone but us, but we know the story by heart; he could tell they understood him and nodded, one of the women even got up from her seat and moved up near him, holding tight to the handles at every curve. She wanted to learn the whole story and asked a bunch of questions, and Papà told me, 'The way she was listening, she must be a journalist, maybe she'll even write something about it. I'm talking and she's swallowing the words, her eyes dancing, I've never seen anything like it.' When they reached the city entrance, he didn't leave them at the stop there, but took them downhill close to the market because they wanted to buy some fruit, and everyone shook his hand. There were no more passengers in the minibus, he looked at them once more before returning to the station and that was the end of it. Why didn't he tell me yesterday so I could bring them here? I might have learned who the woman was who seemed so interested and why she was so excited when she heard our story. But now they're already back home in Ljubljana, that's what they said anyway, although I thought I saw a large group of adults and children that looked like them. When I walked past the Rio Bar, I noticed some people drinking coffee on the terrace, and on the quay a few children were flying blue balloons. It struck me a little odd that they were all holding the same color balloons and the wind was trying to pull them away but the children were running around laughing, music was pouring from the restaurants, and I couldn't hear what language they were shouting. It's too bad. I've always wanted people from your part of the world to come to Castellammare del Golfo, and now, when people really did come who understand your language, the language that, thank God, you taught me, I didn't get a chance to meet them.

I AM SITTING BY HER GRAVE and I'm telling her all this and I know that she's listening attentively to me, waiting for me to fall silent and then she'll say something back. We talk like this every day—I stay silent awhile, then I talk aloud, so long as I'm sure no one will suddenly come out into the garden. Who knows how—but I hear Grandma answer me, her voice sounds the same as when she was healthy and alive. Sometimes she'll talk about various things and then she'll be silent for days. To be honest, no one wanted to hear the same things a hundred times over, except me, and Papà of course. But when he was really tired after driving the minibus, he just wanted to nap, and not listen to Grandma talk yet again about the war, about Split, or even about Sicily. As for Margherita, ever since she was little she had developed a protective mechanism against Grandma's stories—whenever Grandma started in, Margherita simply put her hands over her ears, closed her eyes, and made a loud hissing sound through her teeth: 'shshshsh'. I don't know what annoyed Mamma more, Margherita's shushing or Grandma's chattering, but she would mutter as she left the room, 'Out of spite.' That's how Grandma had only me to listen to her stories about the time before, during, and after the war. First, she spoke in Italian, then later, after Granddad died, she began teaching me Croatian, and after six months she said: 'This is the last time I'm going to speak Italian with you, you know enough of my language for it to be yours as well.' She talked to me and I swallowed up new words, which seemed to me more funny than difficult, and when I got home from school I did almost nothing else, except listen to Grandma Neda, my Nonna Nedjeljka, talk and talk. And the more I understood what Grandma was telling me, the more I felt she belonged to me and the less ashamed I was of the name Nedjeljka. That's why I'm glad we buried her in the garden behind the house. Just like she wanted, just like she told us while she was still alive and alert: 'Now don't you go burying me in the cemetery! I don't plan to be among strangers again when I die.

Bury me wherever you want, but not with other dead people.' We sometimes laughed at her request. Papà once even asked, 'You don't want to be next to my Papà?' Mamma, doubling over with laughter, would leave the room and I'm sure would whisper to herself, as she always did in such situations, 'Out of spite!' 'Carlo and I no longer understand each other,' Grandma replied. 'He doesn't say anything, and I talk.' Once she whispered to me, 'He speaks one language, I speak another.' And when she died, Papà firmly announced that under no circumstance were we going to bury her in the cemetery. 'Either we take her back to Split or we bury her here at home.' Then Mamma told me, 'Go ask around and find out how much it would cost to send a body to Split.' 'Where?' I asked her. 'I don't know, here, or call someone in Split, or maybe the Croatian Embassy in Rome. You can speak Croatian, your Grandma didn't teach it to you for nothing.' There was a hint of irony in her voice, but her eyes were red, so I forgave her. When we found out that a burial like that would cost three times Papà's salary as a driver, Mamma said, 'She wouldn't even want us to bury her in Split. Who would go visit her grave there? Her brother? That old dumbbell with his broken finger? Or that daughter of his who didn't try even once to contact her in her entire life?' And so, in fact, it was Mamma who somehow persuaded us to bury her here in the yard, under the orange tree. In the same place where the rope swing used to be that Granddad had attached for Papà and my uncles, the same spot where, years later, Papà had put a real wooden swing for Margherita and me. Grandma never pushed us on the swing—it was an unwritten rule that this was Granddad's job, but often when we got back from school, we found her sitting on it, without making the slightest movement, like a picture of a woman frozen on a swing —though I don't know if anyone captured such an image or made such a sculpture.

AND NOW, Nonna, now that you're in that world beyond everything that was part of life and you are once again under this tree—our most beloved orange tree that makes our garden beautiful the whole year—perhaps your memory has returned to you. Perhaps in your death the memory of everything that Papà quickly told the tourists has returned to you. Perhaps you again know where you were born and where you lived before you moved here. Do you remember Split? The war? Your mother and father? Your brother? Us? Me, your namesake?

WHILE SHE WAS ALIVE, my Grandma Nedjeljka remembered everything, events of the past and everyday events up through June 2009. Or, more exactly, up to June 7, 2009.

Up to that date, up to my twenty-first birthday, she was still a normal grandmother, mother, and mother-in-law. Old, but normal. Very old, but vital. Grandma and her brother evidently had their mother's genes and could expect to live to ninety. I was turning the age considered a legal adult in America. The orange tree here was blossoming and we were sitting beneath it at the wooden table. I was sitting with Mamma, Papà, Margherita, and her boyfriend—a serious boyfriend—Pietro. He was a full twenty years older than Margherita. She was eighteen, he was thirty-eight. A very pleasant and open guy, but too old! 'He's so old, where did you dig him up?' Grandma would say whenever he left our place. 'Magi's a child, he's an old man!' And she never missed the opportunity to turn to Papà and say, 'Go find Margherita a proper suitor! A young girl shouldn't be going around with an old man!' But for Papà it was even more unpleasant what Margherita dished back: she'd just laugh and say, 'He's young, don't you worry!' and Papà would feel guilty that Margherita had found herself such an old boyfriend. Still, once he even said, 'I guess better old than nothing,' probably alluding to me who, at 21 years of age, had yet to bring a young man home. Margherita had joked with me that day: 'Well, now that Neda's 'forever young,' she doesn't need a man.' 'Which Neda?' Grandma asked, and we all laughed. 'You,' I said to her devilishly, although everyone yelled, 'Neda, not you, you're 86 years old, Neda's only 21. And you're Nedjeljka, Nonna Non-Oui.'

And then, as I clearly recall, Grandma started shouting: 'I'm twenty-one years old! I'm Neda and today is my birthday!' 'But Nonna,' I said trying to calm her, but she screamed at me, 'Nonna?! What do you mean, Nonna? I'm a young woman. I'm twenty-one years old, my name is Neda, my mama has a stand in the market, my father's a fisherman, we live in Split.' 'Of course, of course, that's nice, Mamma,' our father said, trying to smooth things over, but she started in on him, too: 'Mamma? What do you mean Mamma? I am a young woman and I'm not married. Carlo's waiting for me on the Riva!' How strange my birthday was! At first we thought Grandma was joking and we were joking with her, but she wouldn't let up and kept trying to convince us she was the Neda celebrating her birthday, not me. When she couldn't convince us, she began to shout at the top of her lungs, and called us liars, thieves, even fascists. We quickly cleared the dishes and the food from the table in the garden and managed somehow to get her inside. The special Split cake that Grandma had made the day before—working all day in the kitchen, her spattered recipe in front of her—remained in the small refrigerator that Papà had put in the corner of the garden several years earlier. No one even remembered it until days later. I think all of us felt our hearts pounding in our temples. We went inside, closed the door that led to the garden, and shuffled off to our own rooms. Grandma went to her own room as well, repeating over and over as she climbed the stairs: 'Faa-scists. Faa-scists!'

NONNA, why did you call us fascists? In the days that followed, you repeated that word and for the six full years until your death. Why was it that that word poured from your mouth a hundred times a day? Sometimes it would be the only word you said. What really happened that day? An outpouring of pent-up hatred towards all of us, your closest kin, or the final outpouring of illness? Doctor Rinaldo said it was a typical sign of Alzheimer's and had no connection to concrete causes and consequences. You were simply ill. Old and sick. Surely you had been sick a long time, but that day the illness appeared in its truest light. Something flipped the switch on your illness right then on my birthday. 'You were lucky till then. At that age, grandmothers are usually in their graves, in an old folks' home, or seriously ill. Signora Nedjeljka Lombardo has a good heart, but her brain is no longer functioning properly, and it will continue like this from now on,' the doctor said, then added, 'and get worse. Do not leave her alone for a moment.' 'Do we need to sleep with her as well?' Mamma asked sarcastically, then immediately bit her lip. 'No, she can sleep alone, but lock the balcony door, just in case.' It was my job to lock the balcony door to your room every night, then hide the key in my room. How hard it was for me to do that, how hypocritical I felt, showing a granddaughter's love towards you during the day, while at night taking your freedom to the balcony with its lovely view of the belltower beside the Holy Mother of God cathedral. Every evening before I left your room, I kissed your forehead, and you would grab my hand that held the balcony key. 'Faa-scists, Faa-scists,' you repeated with eyes closed, and I felt the palm of my hand sweat as it clenched the key. I felt my heart pounding in my temples, and I hated myself for playing the role of prison guard. The door to your room remained unlocked, and during the night you often went back and forth to the washroom several times, either because you had forgotten to turn off the tap or had completely forgotten to do what you went there for; you just sat there gazing into the night without turning on the light. Meanwhile, in my half of the room, separated from Margherita's by a tall bookshelf, I would think about everything that had happened, how I'd lost you, my Grandma, while you were still alive, and how you knew yourself that you're the most important person in my life. We were as close as 'ass to panties,' as Papà would describe us, and Mamma would not forget to add 'out of spite.'

I ASKED MYSELF whether her illness was somehow connected to Granddad, who had died thirteen long years earlier. 'Alzheimer's defies logic,' Dr. Rinaldo said to me, 'don't try to find reasons for it. It occurs in young people and in old ones.' Yes, it can't be Granddad's fault, he's been dead so many years and is buried, alone, in the city graveyard. He died in 1996 when I was eight and my sister five, but he had been mute for the two years before that because of some undiagnosed medical condition, though Grandma told us it was because he had really wanted to teach my sister and me to swim, and he would take us to the beach, to the bay, any time, whenever the sun was shining, but Margherita and I cried and kicked so much that one day Margherita, the tough little thing, slipped out of his arms and nearly drowned and Granddad barely managed to pull her from the water, shouting at me: 'Step on her back, step on her back!' Still today I feel that I can hear him shouting, as I, a six-year-old, in tears, wet and frozen, climbed crying onto the back of my little sister, who was barely three years old. I stepped on her, and from her mouth poured gurgling water and a cry, a cry that could be heard by every person in Castellammare del Golfo, and from that moment he never spoke again; he went mute over night, he never took us to the beach again, and whenever anyone asked him something, he simply could not answer—only odd mumbling and gurgling sounds came out of his mouth. My father and uncles took him everywhere they could think of, beginning with the small clinic here where they knew him as Carlo, with that wife of his, Nedjeljka, Neda, from Yugoslavia. The first question the nurse asked was, 'Did the Mafia do anything to him,' but since the answer was negative, the doctor, the only one in the clinic, had no other answer to explain why my grandfather had so abruptly stopped talking, but said only 'He's had a fright, it will pass. He just needs time.' But when the 'time' that passed was a whole year following Margherita's near drowning with its happy ending, Uncle Mario, who lived in Trieste, sent a ticket to Granddad to sail to Trieste, where he would take him to the best doctor in the city, 'the American,' my uncle wrote. 'He'll surely know what to do.' My Granddad set off for Trieste, alone, unused to traveling with anyone, on his first trip since the war, while Grandma, even though she wanted to visit her son in Trieste, was in the end, overcome with fear and stayed home, wringing her hands beneath her apron as she waited for the pasta spread out on the white tablecloth to dry in the only empty room in the house, the one that had been Uncle Mario's. But not even in Trieste was there a cure for Granddad's muteness. Uncle Mario even sent him on to Rome, to their younger brother's, Uncle Luca and Uncle Luca went with Granddad from doctor to doctor, hospital to hospital, but they all said the same thing: 'He's had a fright and been struck mute, he just needs time for the fear to pass, and then he'll begin to speak again.' However, there was a nurse in the suburbs of Rome, who had earlier been a client at Uncle Luca's law office, who took my uncle aside and said to him, 'As you know, I'm not from here, but I know how to drive away fear: you take an axe, the person who has suffered this fright sits in the doorway to the house facing outside, and then the person who's the head of the household takes the axe and swings it in the doorway right beside the sick person saying, 'Fear, leave this house, because, only without fear can a person be a person.' You do that three times—on the person's right side and their left, and once in the air over his head—and you'll see how the fear leaves him.' That's what she said to my Uncle Luca to help Granddad Carlo talk again like before: 'That's what people do where I come from. I don't know about how they do it where you're from, but why not give it a try? It doesn't cost anything to try.' Uncle Luca put a sheet of paper in Granddad's suitcase on which he had written the nurse's advice with a p.s.: Mamma, maybe you'd understand these things, the nurse is an immigrant from Yugoslavia.'

AH NEDI, we didn't have that custom in Split, but I had heard about it. A long time ago, when I was a little girl, I read a book of folk stories from the Kingdom of Yugoslavia, and in one of them I read something like that; it upset me so much that I though about the story all night: a woman had gone off to live with her husband's family after she got married, and she was very afraid of his sister, who was an evil woman and one day her husband cut her fear with an axe right in the doorway to their house. Then she and her sister-in-law became like sisters. But the sister-in-law soon got married and moved away. I thought about this story while I was reading the advice from the hospital nurse in Rome, and I thought we should give it a try, but your Granddad wouldn't hear of such a thing to drive out his fear and he just shook his head and ran out of the room. I think the problem was also that he was the head of the house, and it would have been devastating if all at once his son took over that role while his father was still living. But it was also 'out of spite,' your mama said, when she thought I wasn't listening. He didn't let us do it, even though I thought it was the only thing that could save Carlo. I stroked his head, but he silently pushed my hand away, because he didn't want our tenderness or our help and none of us were brave enough to just put him in the doorway and cut away the fear that had taken his voice. He died in his sleep two years later, you were eight by then, and Margherita was five, and hadn't said a word for 24 months. He just sat there mute in our marriage bed, in the rocking chair on the balcony, here at the table under the orange tree, and in the armchair in the living room. Gaping open-mouthed at the television as if every second he had something he wanted to say but couldn't. He said nothing to me before he died. Nothing. He passed away in silence, leaving me with countless unspoken words.

NONNA, that morning, the day you were supposed to go to Split again after the last time you went, nearly thirty years before, Grandad Carlo simply didn't wake up. I remember, it was 1996 because that was the year I started second grade, and Margherita was still at home. You and Granddad took care of her, and when I got home from school, we would make paper airplanes from the pages of *La Sicilia* and we would fly them all over the house. We'd peek again and again into the drawer in your room where, hidden in a silk-covered box like a precious stone, was the airplane ticket my uncles and Papà had bought so you could go to Split. Later you told me you had decided to go that year, 1996, because it had been announced on the RAI Italian news broadcast that all military action had ended in the former Yugoslavia and there was no more shooting, those who had fought in Croatia received the title 'defenders,' and that the war just ended had been called a 'patriotic' one; you told me that the president of Croatia was shown on the breaking news for several seconds holding up a *Law on Croatian Homeland War Veterans and Members of Their Families*, and you felt uncomfortable, as if he had done something to you personally. I don't remember that news broadcast. Margherita and I surely had more interesting things to do. I know we had to make a hangar for all the little airplanes because Mamma threatened to throw them all in the trash because they were underfoot everywhere including the bathroom. Now, as I think about it, I think the situation in Croatia wasn't exactly clear to you either, and even less so to Mamma and Papà, but who knows, maybe Papà knew exactly what was going on in your homeland—though he once told me that he simply didn't want to know anything so it would be easier for you. I do remember your fear during the war in Yugoslavia, when images of military strikes were broadcast on Italian television, your face, and Granddad Carlo's, would crumple and you wouldn't blink for hours, your lips tightly pursed as if glued together. 'Look, Grandma's a doll,' Margherita said to me, but to me you looked like the models I had once seen in one of the classrooms where a teacher sent me to get chalk. I walked into the room and screamed terrified: there, standing on the tables, were several anatomic models and a skeleton. They were all gross and frightening with organs hanging on small hooks. There was one body that was not completely terrifying: one with a partial left cheek, an eye, the left-half of a nose, and half a mouth. The other side wasn't there, so these parts of the face were clearly visible, hanging on small hooks at the mid-point of the head. The eye was open, as was one nostril, but the upper and lower mouth were glued shut, and, if the right side of the face had been there, its lips would also have been glued shut as well. 'It doesn't blink and doesn't breathe,' I told Margherita, as I explained to her what I had seen for the first time in my life, and she said, 'Just like Grandma.' You often looked like that: eyes wide open, nostrils flared, lips sealed shut; you were so frightened by events in your homeland that came at you like a news flash, and so worried about your home in Split, about your brother who hadn't contacted you even once, not even when his wife, a Serbian, died, and your niece who never made the effort to get in touch with you. You were convinced that it must be the same there as it had been during the second world war, during the time of your war—as you would say to us, then always correcting yourself: 'Your granddad's war.' Yet, perhaps now more than ever before, you wanted to go to Split to see with your own eyes the traces of this new war, to feel in person the new peace, and we all hastened to fulfil your wish— Margherita and I with our paper airplanes, Papà and our uncles with a real round-trip plane ticket: Trapani-Trieste-Split and back. No one told you not to go, or asked what you were looking for in a country that had just been through a war, where there was likely still some shooting even though no one talked about it anymore, it was as if we were the ones who wanted at any cost to send you among the stray bullets fired by traumatized defenders and attackers, even if you never came back. But Granddad Carlo didn't wake up that morning, so you didn't go then or ever. You took Granddad's death as a sign that you no longer needed to go to Split at least once more to see your home, your brother, your niece, the only ones left in your family, and you kept repeating that, after settling in Castellammare del Golfo in 1947, it was your fate to return to your native country only two times: the first in 1959, the second and final time in 1968. You said to me many times: 'Ah, Nedi, when you no longer live somewhere, you're dead to that place. And when a dead person returns to where she was once alive, it is as a ghost. And everyone is afraid of ghosts, right? Children and grownups.' Your words didn't make sense to me. I couldn't understand why you were already dead where you no longer live; you simply live in another place, and sometimes you travel to where you lived before—for my generation, traveling has become the most normal thing, a tourist destination, not an existential question. And, no, not everyone would be afraid of you if they saw you. I, for one, wouldn't be afraid of you if I lived in Split and you turned up unexpectedly. And why shouldn't people who love us want to see us again? Even if we are ghosts? When you were in Split you were a young girl, a living human being, you had girlfriends. But fate wanted you to fall in love with an Italian. Can it be that love, which believes in everything and has hope in everything, turns people into ghosts when they move to a new place to follow their loved ones?

AH, NEDI, Saint Paul neglected to put that in his epistle to the Corinthians. But he most likely didn't know that a person who loves someone and leaves her home country on account of that love, becomes a ghost because of it. It's worth remembering that she also lives like a ghost in her new country as well. The person becomes like domestic spirits which the people living in the house and those around them gradually fear less and less, yet they still look at the newcomer differently, as if the person had something stuck to her head or clothes, as if she were marked in some way. They seemed to look at me like that on those rare occasions when Carlo had too much to do in the workshop and I had to help, even though he'd told me when I moved here: 'We'll live on my shoemaker's salary. There's no need for you to work, you don't know the language well enough. Besides, you never know who's going to turn up at the workshop. The Mafiosi also wear shoes, after all, and what shoes! But if you want, you can sew upstairs in our place above the shop.' It was rare those years for Carlo and me to go to the Rosetti store or take a short walk to the bay. Of course, those were years when a woman didn't walk about town alone, but at that time when there were whispers of more gunfights, a man didn't either. It wasn't just me, a foreigner, a woman unfamiliar with the Mafia's laws, it was also the other women who didn't leave their houses; we just peeked through the curtains. We were all ghosts, those of us who had come from somewhere else and the locals. But in my native country, if the ghost of a woman were to reappear either no one would recognize her any longer and would not see her as either a living person or as a ghost, while everyone who did recognize her would compare her with the way she had looked before and would simply not see her as anything but a ghost. I don't know if you understand at all what I'm telling you. If you were to move somewhere, you would understand what I'm talking about. If it's because you love someone, it will be easier for you. Easier no matter how hard it is. Just like it was for me after '47. Let me tell you something even more important and more truthful: it's likely better to be a ghost because of love than because of war. Not war like on television or in a movie about a war but war right where you live. To be a witness to war. It begins with a feeling, a premonition, then unusual signs and signals, then moves on to the explosions. You live normally, and suddenly the world collapses. Can you imagine? Can you imagine that in 1939 I would ever have imagined that within the span of two years all these things would happen? In Split and in the rest of the world.

ACCORDING TO MY GRANDMA, the most important event in Split in June 1939 was the arrival of a huge tourist ship from France. She was sixteen. While it was strange for her, it was even stranger for her nine-year old brother. For the older people it wasn't that special: in the summer of 1936 they had seen a flood of tourists come to Split from Czechoslovakia on charter planes from Prague. The Czech tourists blended in with the locals and didn't stand out because of their clothes or their demeanor. The people could even understand each other's languages somewhat, so those tourists didn't cause shock waves in Split. But the news that a boat full of French tourists had arrived—each Parisian more elegantly dressed than the last—spread through the city faster than lightening. 'Thank God they're not Germans,' whispered the locals, the older and more educated among them who already recognized the direction Germany was headed. Grandma Neda's girlfriends shouted so loudly for her to go out with them that she thought something terrible had happened. They didn't explain why they were shouting, just laughed and called out *no-yes* in French, 'Non-Oui! Non-Oui!' as her French teacher often called her and pulled her through the narrow streets from the old town towards the Riva and the port where, in her alarm and fear, Grandma didn't even notice the ship occupying *the whole sea* as the locals later described it. All she saw was her brother Krsto, and she ran to him, thinking something terrible had happened to him. But Krsto stood frozen on the shore, open-mouthed, and didn't notice his sister tugging him by the elbow. He only noticed when his hand let go of the handkerchief their mother had ironed that morning with the flat iron, hot from the stove, and given him to wipe his runny nose. Only then did he see her and say, 'Leave me alone.' One after another, the ladies and gentlemen stepped from the boat in summer hats and silk dresses, with leather bags and valises. There were tourists who'd come to Split in those years, but there had never been such a large group from France. The captain helped each woman off the ship, but the men who accompanied them also held their elbow. The last to descend was a young woman dressed in red slacks, a white blouse, and a red scarf with white dots that was interlaced with the strap of her camera, a type Grandma had never seen before. Her curly hair fell to her shoulders. She carried a handbag, a suitcase, and a large notebook that looked like a ship's log. She appeared to be alone, since no one offered to take her suitcase, except for the captain helping her off the ship, and the harbour porters. She paused a moment on the Riva, looked around, and when she caught sight of Krsto waving the small whitish hand-kerchief intended for his nose, she smiled broadly at him and gestured with her finger for him to come over. But Grandma held him tight by the elbow. She was still afraid and confused for reasons she couldn't explain. But Krsto pushed her away and ran towards the woman in slacks. She handed him the large notebook and motioned for him to follow her. Grandma wanted to run after them, but her girlfriends pulled her towards the narrow streets saying, 'Let him go, he's just a boy. It's something interesting for him and maybe he'll bring a coin or two back this evening.' Even though this didn't set her mind at ease, she set off with them for home. Her father hadn't returned from fishing, and her mother was still at the market, selling the sardines he'd caught the day before. Their house smelled of fish day and night, just like the houses of all the other fishermen in the old part of town. She found herself all alone on the downstairs' floor where they lived, and she didn't know what to do with herself. While there was always housework to be done and no time to be thinking of such things, she considered going upstairs to her

aunt and uncle's—relatives with whom she hadn't spoken for
years—to work things out between them once and for all, even
though she'd never quarreled with them herself. Instead, she sat
down by the window and looked out at the Church of the Holy
Cross while images of all those French people descending from
the ship danced in her head. The jumble of people—who was
the best dressed, most beautiful, most fashionable? And then
there was that woman at the end who'd called her brother to
help her with the ship's log or whatever that large, hard-covered
notebook was. She was unusual, the only one in slacks, the only
one alone. No traveling companion, no husband, no dog, no one.
Was it possible to set off from France and sail for days like that
alone, all by yourself, like she did? My grandmother told herself
that there was nothing worse in this life than being alone, even
if you were from Paris.

AH, NEDI, Krsto didn't come home that day for lunch and still
wasn't back by evening. At around ten o'clock, my mother sent
me out looking for him. She said, 'Since you're the one who
didn't stop him from going off with those tourists, go find him
yourself.' Papa only nodded. I went out into our neighborhood
and down along the Riva. I was afraid of the dark and the dogs
barking nearby and off in the distance, but there were a lot
of people on the Riva, mostly from the ship, and I looked for
my brother among them, but he wasn't there. Then I saw him
out on the dock sitting with the French woman and my high
school French teacher. They looked like a picture of a family as
I approached: she was beautiful, all dressed up, wrapped in a
red sweater made of some strange fabric I'd never seen before.
My teacher looked different than he did in class. His hair was
slicked back, most likely rubbed with olive oil, and my brother
held the large notebook in his hands and was sitting between
them. My heart was pounding when I stopped in front of them.
'Krsto, come home, we've been waiting all day for you,' I said. My

teacher quickly said: 'Nedjeljka, Non-Oui, you should begin by saying good evening. Meet Miss Charlotte Guillet from Paris, a journalist with *Le Figaro*. Krsto will be her assistant while she's here. I'll be her interpreter.' I extended my hand to the woman and quietly said, 'Nedjeljka,' but my teacher corrected me immediately: 'Ne-da' he stretched the name out and said to Charlotte, '*Ne-da, non-oui,* that's what we call her in my class because *ne* is the local word for the French *non,* and *da* is *oui.*' Charlotte laughed aloud, gave me her hand and, seemed to want to say something to me but only managed to repeat, 'Non-Oui.' Krsto quickly got up, slipped the ship log into her lap, and pulled me away. 'Tomorrow, right after school,' my teacher called after him. 'Don't make us wait for you!' Krsto and I nearly ran home, me angry at him and him at me. In front of the house, I couldn't stop myself from pulling his hair and giving him a slap. 'Mama yelled at me!' I shouted. 'Because of you! I had to walk the entire Riva to find you! You idiot!' But he gave back as good as he got, and he bit my wrist. I knew he hadn't liked me from the moment he was born. The first time they put him in my arms, he began to cry and turn red, so my mother took him right back. Whenever I held him, that is whenever he was given to me to hold—I was seven and could hold a baby—he'd start screaming so loudly that I wanted to drop him and let him see how that felt. We hadn't liked each other at first sight and still didn't. Maybe it was the seven-year age difference that separated us from the very start. He spent several days after school with the French woman and my teacher, and, when she left aboard the ship, she left him so much money that he, a nine-year old, bought himself a used bicycle. He didn't keep it out in the yard but carried it to our room and, out of spite, as your mother would say, parked it by my bed.

BUT CHARLOTTE DID RETURN just two months later, on a different ship, a passenger ship, several days' travel from France. She arrived with six suitcases, an enormous hatbox, and a journalist's leather briefcase of a sort that not even the educated men in Split had, not to mention women her age. Grandma's teacher waited for her at the port. French classes that year began with French love songs. What grammar, what tenses! The students sang, laughed, and practiced. Grandma's school had never been so much fun. She even got the lead role in Jean-Jacques Bernard's play *Martine*. As for Krsto, he didn't leave his bike for an instant. He even rode it to the neighbours, brought it into the yard, into the house, where he leaned it against his sister's bed, which really annoyed her. During the day she forgot about it and around the house she even absent-mindedly sang the French melodies she was learning at school. Her mother wondered aloud, 'What has come over my children ever since that French woman muddled their brains?' And the day Krsto rushed into the room and shouted 'Charlotte's back! With six suitcases!' everyone clearly knew right away that she was there to stay. 'She's a fool,' their mother said, 'to move from Paris to Split!' 'From a horse to a donkey!' That's what the whole city was saying. 'She's a journalist, educated, beautiful, young, modern, from Paris, that's right, from Paris!' No one was very happy about Charlotte's move to Split, but they figured it was a direct result of her first trip there. 'That teacher likely pumped her up. He looks all fine and cultured, but it turns out he's a womanizer!' But no one could detect any signs that Charlotte was pregnant, not after the teacher and the French woman's small intimate wedding or during the entire year that followed. Her slender body drew sighs from unmarried and married alike along the Riva. When she walked hand-in-hand with him, her hair down and her body straight as a ship's mast, the men were excited by the mere sight of her, and during those months, said Grandma, quietly laughing, you could hear moans from many houses in Split. At home Krsto talked about how there was something strange going on in the city: while riding his bicycle, he could hear a lot of moaning voices behind windows.

This made Neda's face flush, and their mother's, and their father would leave the room, but those muffled sounds came from their bedroom, too, waking Grandma, and half-asleep she'd say, 'I can't move a muscle without waking Krsto,' as she pictured her mother and her father—his left foot shorter than his right since birth—joined together, one on top of the other, moaning and groaning. When Charlotte did give birth to Marcel in 1942, gunshots could be heard throughout the city and not only were the windows shut, but the shutters as well, and it seemed that no one in Split was moaning with passion any longer.

NO, NONNA. I read a study about how even in wartime people need passion, they need sex. Even more so than during normal times: it's a kind of anti-stress therapy—relaxation and enjoyment. Still, when there's shooting going on outside, people are ashamed to moan with pleasure, and they're afraid. It must have been like that for Charlotte and your teacher since they most likely conceived their son in April 1941, maybe before April 10 when Croatia declared itself the Independent State of Croatia, with Ante Pavelić as its head. Many Italian soldiers and some German ones marched through the city, and the Croatians who saw themselves in the image of the Ustashi did not hesitate to inflict pain on anyone who looked at them askance or stood up to them. A few days earlier, the Italians who had always lived in Split and Dalmatia began to leave their homes and depart for Italy *en masse*. As for Charlotte, instead of fleeing with your teacher to France on one of the ships leaving the harbour, she stayed in Split. She was pregnant, and it didn't occur to her to suggest to her husband that they leave Split before things got even worse. At least that was Krsto's terse answer when at home you asked him whether he had seen Charlotte. All he could tell you was that she and the French teacher were now living in the basement of their house, along with his parents. The upper floors were empty, heavy curtains blocked the windows, and the shutters were nailed shut. You didn't go to school any longer. The last year of high school simply remained an open book, a notebook left unwritten. Every war closes schools and opens graveyards. And in between: hiding, hunger, poverty, and fear.

AH NEDI, God grant that you never know what war is. What hunger is. Your stomach rumbles day and night, and there you are, a young woman, hungry and thirsty for bread and for life. Anything of value that we had at home was traded little by little for eggs, bread, a chicken, a piece of bacon. The overcoat Papa had bought one cold winter in the twenties went, and so did Mama's fur stole that she'd brought from Rijeka as part of her trousseau. Mama cried when Papa wanted to go fishing, and she reminded him that a single bullet from those Italian dogs was enough to put an end to everything. He'd be dead. We'd be left orphans and she'd be a widow. 'Let your brother go. It's not so hard on him,' she would say, alluding to the fact that my uncle had no children. She cried loudly and kept shouting, so Papa, mainly from the shame he felt from his brother, who lived on the floor above us, no longer left the house. I'm not sure where he managed to hide when soldiers arrived looking to conscript him. Right after the bombing of Belgrade when the occupation of Yugoslavia began, my uncle went off with some people from the Regional Committee, without so much as a word, without saying goodbye, but Papa—who once said it was no good being a communist, fascist, member of the Ustashi, or fifth-column traitor, and who also didn't recognize either independent Croatia or the Kingdom of Yugoslavia—did not go. He disappeared for three days, and we wondered where he was, and whether he had also gone off with someone. But who? He turned up on the third night completely blackened with charcoal. 'I'm not back from anywhere, I've been home the whole time, in the chimney,' he said, which struck me as funny—he looked like a chimney sweep. I immediately grabbed a button on the shirt I was wearing because the superstition says if you grab your button when you see a chimney sweep, your wish will come true. That summer when, like every other summer, we had cucumbers and tomatoes growing in our garden, Mama said that, despite everything, she was going to the market to sell a few kilos, but Papa screamed at her not to go anywhere. We would eat the cucumbers and tomatoes ourselves because the children needed a mother, and she knew quite well that all it took was a single bullet and that would be the end; he'd be a widower and the children orphans. That's how they protected one another, by shouting and threatening. I realized then that love had a prickly side and that there were times when you had to be mean to protect the ones you loved. So we pretty much stayed home, and when there was shooting nearby, or when bombers flew overhead, we ran down to the cellar where my aunt would soon join us. My aunt and uncle didn't have children, but I knew she'd had two miscarriages. She and my mother had had a fight and were estranged. Something similar had happened to nearly every other family we knew, always for stupid reasons, but in our family, it was because Papa had left his fishing boots off to the side, near the foot of the stairs my aunt and uncle used to go up to their apartment, rather than leaving them directly in front of our entry door. And one night my aunt came down to do her business in the toilet we shared out in the yard and tripped over the boots, fell, and miscarried, losing her second pregnancy. That led to a bitter quarrel between my mother and my aunt, although, really, it was Papa's fault, but at that time it was quite clear and considered normal that women were responsible for everything, especially things relating to the men, and if Mama had just moved Papa's fishing boots closer to our door, Auntie wouldn't have fallen and miscarried. During those years Papa and his brother would exchange a word or two, but not the women, and both Krsto and I were forbidden to speak with Auntie down in the shelter. We were forced to sit there together without a word, gloomy and anxious because of the blasts we heard outside. Even though we were related, we were greater enemies to one another than we were to our enemies, the Ustashi, Italians, and Germans. Maybe it's because we were so silent in the cellar that they never found us, not even when they rushed into the house and searched every room. Krsto had had the idea of covering the opening leading to the cellar with a sewer lid so no one would think there was a cellar under it rather than a hole. 'How did you come up with that, Krsto?' Mama asked him, and he said, 'That's what they do at Yuri's.' The last person to go down would pull the cover over, without saying a word. Inside, we sat in silence, the women filled with hatred and anger, disgusted with one another. Krsto would listen to the shooting, Papa sat with his head in his hands, while I, as always, literally always, thought about the child, the boy or girl cousin that Auntie would have had if she hadn't tripped over Papa's rubber boots tossed carelessly in front of their stairs.

KRSTO WAS HUNGRY, just like everyone else, but for an 11-year-old it meant he was also angry at the whole world and began running off every afternoon and returning before the curfew, the *coprifuoco,* as it was called in Italian. Towards the middle of June, he brought home a can of oil and a can of lard from the barrack's warehouse. Two weeks later they were all woken by raps at the door, but they didn't answer. The pounding then moved on to the door upstairs, at Auntie's. She shouted at them, 'What lard, I didn't take any lard!' and shortly after that, the footsteps on the stairs fell silent. Krsto rarely came home now empty-handed from his meanderings around the city. Sometimes he brought an unopened can of food, sometimes an open can of some kind of thick soup or other, or a hunk of bread, or several slices of zwieback. The cans were Italian, a kind only the Ustashi could buy at that time. His mother and father didn't ask where he'd got them or from whom: probably an Ustashi, Italian, or German soldier. They were all enemies, but the food that Krsto brought home was tasty, and it was sometimes the only food they tasted the entire day. Grandma would keep asking where he got the cans, where he went every day, where he was wandering about, why his bicycle was banged up, and why he got back home at the same time every evening. Krsto would either stubbornly keep his mouth shut or just say, 'What's it to you? Keep your nose in your own business!' She didn't have any of her own business, so she looked after his. One day, instead of food, he brought home a French fashion catalogue dated 1939. 'Charlotte gave it to me,' he said right off. 'She found it in a box, and since it's also got patterns inside, she told me you might be able to sew something.' He said this to his mother, but it was his sister who couldn't take her eyes off the brightly-coloured dress on the cover. She grabbed the catalogue from his hands, and the patterns, which made up almost half the catalogue, fell out. There were patterns for dresses, skirts, and slacks. This was the first time in their lives she and her mother had seen patterns for women's pants. While girls had worn pants in Split since before the war, she'd never imagined that there were patterns for them. Thanks to that catalogue from Charlotte, things between Grandma and her brother settled down a bit, until the day when she couldn't stand being at home any longer and decided to set out after him to see where he went every afternoon. There was only sporadic gunfire that day, and it seemed calmer than other days. From a distance, Grandma secretly tailed Krsto, who had developed a strategy for moving around, ducking through small streets, then dashing like lightening along the wider streets where there was nowhere to hide. Now, with his sister, dashing breathlessly behind him, he reached the Hotel Park on Bačvice Beach, the enemy headquarters where the Bergamo, the 15th Italian division, was stationed. The guard smiled and let him pass, then waved to Grandma for her to come, too. When she saw where Krsto was going and the soldier waving to her, she got frightened, turned around, and set off at a run back along the same streets and alleyways, more disturbed than ever. She had the feeling that the soldier who was standing in front of the headquarters was running after her and would grab her and shoot at any second. That evening when Krsto got home, all she said to him was, 'Come, let me show you something,' and she pulled him into their room and threw a blanket over him and began smothering him, shouting, 'You son of a bitch! You god-damned son of a bitch! You've been going to them! You fascist! Fascist!'

AH, NEDI, I was eighteen years old with no present, no future, and the past was like a little pebble kicked along Split's cobblestone streets. Now that I'd figured out where my brother was going, I couldn't stand it. The only thing that kept me from smothering him in the blanket, was Papa, who came rushing into the room. 'Hey,' he shouted, 'let me sing you children a song I learned from Hrvoje. He says all the Partisans are singing it.' He sang 'Marjane Marjane,' and then said, 'It's a new song. Someone just made it up, one of us, a Croatian, someone from Split. About our Marjan Hill!' There was excitement, joy, and fear in his voice. I had stopped squeezing Krsto under the blanket, and he emerged crying, red-faced, then bit me on the wrist as hard as he could. His teeth were no longer soft baby teeth but more like an animal's, nourished by cans of fascist food. 'Neda's trying to suffocate me,' he shouted jumping from the bed, 'She's trying to kill me!' but neither Mama nor Papa believed him. In their eyes, I was a dear and loving daughter, without the strength to do such things. 'Every afternoon Krsto's been going to Bačvice, to the fascists,' I shot back, and then Papa forgot about everything, the song about Marjan Hill, his brother off with the Partisans, who surely sang that song, and the question going round his head for some time, whether he too should also join them. Everything stopped. 'You've been going to Bačvice?' he repeated hoarsely. 'To the Italian headquarters?' 'Yes,' said Krsto. 'But I'm not doing anything bad. I just sing, I sing them songs from Split, Dalmatian songs. That's why they give me food. Where else could I be getting food like that?' 'That's where you're getting the food?' Mama said, as if it had just dawned on her that the canned goods were Italian. 'No, I buy them at the store,' Krsto shouted sarcastically at her. 'All you do is sing for them?' I managed to ask him without raising my voice. 'Yes, what else would I do? I just sing, in Croatian. Yuri sings in Russian. 'Yuri. Who's Yuri?' Papa asked. 'Yuri! Vladimir's son. Vladimir's the guy who lives in the little house by the palace. Yuri sings in Russian, and he knows how to play the accordion. They give him food, too, sometimes more than they give me.' So that's it, I told myself. He and Yuri sing for the fascists. Yuri was a young Russian, two years younger than my brother, a good-looking kid with blond hair and blue eyes. Up until the war, whenever my girlfriends and I saw him, I'd pinch his cheeks, and they'd stroke his hair. He was the son of a Russian immigrant who had set off alone for Yugoslavia when he was just seventeen to find a refuge from the conditions in Russia after the Revolution. He brought with him two bags of money that his parents had given him, so he'd have something to live on. For months he walked, rode on horseback, traveled by whatever means he could to get to Yugoslavia. He first got off a ship on the island of Vis, but he couldn't live on the island; he wasn't used to having water all around him, so he headed for Split, rented a room, and years later fell in love with his landlord's daughter, Ivana, someone he'd literally grown up with all those years. They got married and he stayed. They had Yuri and then two girls. Even though their mother was from Split, all three of the children, Yuri and his two younger sisters, learned Russian from their father. There are things in your genes you can't overlook, things you can't forget, that inexorably pull you towards whatever it is that's in your blood. Just like me, I've been drawn my whole life to our way of life in Split, and it's like I'm there, but I'm not. Well, the fact was that I now knew Krsto and Yuri were feeding our families with fascist food by singing songs about youth, and love, and our fatherland to the Italian soldiers. That day I stopped eating it.

There had been so much shooting and so many tremors that morning that I thought our house would collapse on our heads any second, but by evening everything had calmed down. It was so quiet that I just walked out of our house. I was drawn outside, to get some air, take a short walk. On the street, I met Yulia, who'd had the same thought. 'Come on, let's go for a walk!' I said and we started laughing, as if the very idea of walking was a joke. We laughed quietly, out of anxiety and fear, our faces furrowed by the thought that someone could shoot from one side or another, the Italians, the Ustashi or the Germans, depending on the mood they were in. Then we caught site of Krsto and Yuri returning from Bačvice. 'Look at them!' Yulia said to me, as her jaw and mine dropped at what we saw. My brother was walking in a coquettish way, perhaps imitating Charlotte, stepping one foot in front of the other, while balancing a round loaf of bread on his head. This was the first time he was bringing home a whole loaf—usually it was just the ends or dried-out crusts. A whole round loaf, which he was carrying on his head, no less! As for Yuri, he marched in front of him singing a Russian love song. They were behaving in a rather peculiar way, a bit sexy for children. Krsto took the bread off his head, pulled it towards his pants, while thrusting his body as if he intended to poke the bread with his penis. 'God, that's gross!' Yulia said while I turned red with embarrassment. 'Krsto!' I shouted at him, without thinking that someone might hear who shouldn't. Krsto froze, along with Yuri. The two of them began running as if they were being chased by soldiers and not by Yulia and me. I turned immediately to head back home, leaving Yulia standing there. When I got home, I ripped into him as harshly as I could, then took the kitchen knife and carved the letter *I* into the loaf of bread which, in the uproar, he had neglected to split with Yuri. 'Now, just go ahead and eat it,' I shouted at him; I would no longer touch the bread. Mama and Papa ate pieces of it without even asking why the initial *I*, for Italy, was carved in it. Krsto wasn't able to bite me again, but he hated me for the rest of my life. From then on, he and I rarely exchanged a single word, just an occasional yes or no. 'Out of spite,' your mother would say. One day, somewhere near the end of 1942, not even a whole hour after leaving the house, Krsto came back with his head bloodied and the pinky on his left hand broken and dangling. What a sight that was. He was shouting in such pain that even Auntie came downstairs. She was living up there alone now, ever since Uncle had gone off to join the Partisans, and even though she said nothing and looked as crazed as the rest of us, she was the first to pull herself together. She ran upstairs and returned with a bottle of iodine. She rubbed Krsto from head to toe, not just where he was bleeding, while he rolled his eyes, half unconscious, in pain and terror. For two days, I didn't know whether he was asleep or in a coma, but none of us woke him, though we each went into the room several times. While it was the room he and I shared, I didn't sleep there those nights because my aunt, without a word, led me upstairs and settled me in their empty room, the room that had been planned for children. On the third day, Krsto opened his eyes and asked Mama, 'Am I alive?' I couldn't help smiling, because despite how much we teased each other and hated each other, we never wished for each other to die, because despite everything, we were brother and sister, of the same mother and father.

WHEN KRSTO HAD HIS STRENGTH BACK more or less, he explained how he'd gone, as usual with Yuri to the Italian headquarters in Bačvice to entertain the soldiers. As usual, he and Yuri sang the same songs, but now Yuri played Dalmatian songs along with the Russian ones on his accordion. And, as usual, the soldiers listened, and sang along a bit. They knew the words by heart after so many identical musical performances. But then, suddenly, one of the soldiers who'd been lying there holding a bottle of alcohol, most likely some sort of fruit brandy, jumped to his feet. He swayed back and forth and began shouting: 'I've had enough of you, you pieces of crap! It's been two years of the same songs! Haven't you learned a single Italian song, a single Sicilian one? You have no idea what music is, what a Sicilian melody is! Is this why we're giving you cans of food and feeding you and your families back at home? You haven't learned a single new song, it's all the same.' This wasn't completely true. Yuri and Krsto had added in a few Italian songs, but they always sang everything they knew, and the soldier, blind drunk, began to spit his drink at them and spilled some straight out of the bottle onto Yuri's accordion. Krsto agreed to sing a new song. And he began to sing 'Marjane, Marjane.' The soldiers even liked the melody, but someone shouted that was the song the Partisans sing and in the last battle he was in, one of them died with that song on his lips. That's just what the soldiers needed. First they laughed, then they teased them, and then they began to kick them and beat them. They yanked the accordion from Yuri's hands and began to hit them with it. Someone took a stone and drilled it into Yuri's head, and, while Krsto was defending him, the soldier with the bottle grabbed hold of Krsto's left hand with something that looked like a bottle opener, and smashed his little finger as hard as he could. After they had savagely beaten them—Krsto had stood there crying silently for half an hour as if he wanted to hold something inside and forget his humiliation, it was so painful—the soldiers drove them out of the camp. Krsto's bicycle was left behind at the headquarters forever. And that was that. Krsto's finger stayed twisted for the rest of his life, and neither he nor Yuri ever went to the Fascists' headquarters again. Italian canned goods never appeared in their homes again. And now the hunger was much worse than at the beginning of the war.

THAT WAS WHY Grandma began to study the patterns from the French fashion catalogue more seriously. She'd sit silently with Auntie on the bed as they looked at the patterns, rotated them, measured them. Auntie still seemed angry at Grandma's family but was softening slowly. Still, Grandma decided to speak only when asked something. At the beginning of their friendship, all she would answer was yes or no. But that didn't inhibit their search of the house for the two forgotten chests Auntie's mother-in-law had left her in which they found several bales of fabric which had likely been there since the twenties. They began to sew, not the dresses and skirts in the magazine patterns, but, as if by unspoken agreement, Partisan pants, shirts, and military caps. They sewed them for uncle and his comrades. Then Grandma Neda felt that even she had something to contribute to the antifascist war.

BUT YOU, NONNA, you didn't want to talk about the war years. You didn't want to and neither did Granddad Carlo. It was as if you had agreed you wouldn't talk about the years he served in the occupying army and you were living at home, moving between the basement and the floor where your aunt lived. You hadn't received a single word from your uncle. Your aunt took the clothes she'd sewn with you to a friend whose husband was also in the Partisans but in a different battalion, and he got the clothes through some other young man, and then divided them among the combatants. Once, you suggested to your aunt that Krsto should take the clothes; he was younger and quicker and had more experience running and escaping than she did and also, as a mature woman she could be caught at night not just by a bullet but also by an enemy's hand. At first Krsto didn't want to. He was afraid he'd run into one of the Italian soldiers he knew from the headquarters and that'd be the end of him. But then Yuri turned up at your house still sporting a bruise over his eye from that drunken night with the Italian soldiers, and you told him your idea. He was delighted he could help the Partisans and said there was no need to take the clothes to your aunt's friend since they could be taken directly to a place where someone from the battalion would wait for them. Krsto gave in and together they took away the clothes you sewed. They'd often hear shots as they ran through the streets. I'm amazed you would even have thought of such a thing, Nonna—sending Krsto on such a risky nighttime adventure. He was a child, and you were already a grown woman. How could you have so little feeling for your brother that you'd risk his life? Your aunt was already used to running through the alleyways, sneaking to her friend's house. And if a bullet had struck her, it wouldn't have been as tragic as if it had happened to Krsto, your only brother. You hadn't received any news from your uncle, and in town there were some who said he had deserted and fled to the Italians; someone claimed to have seen him running into the camp at Bačvice. Your aunt didn't believe it. She said he was too honorable a Croat to do something like that. And there was no one you could send to find out the truth. It would have been easy while Krsto and Yuri were still going to sing in the Italian camp. Others said he'd been shot in a battle near Sinj, along with other Partisans who'd fallen into the hands of the Italians and the Ustashi. A third group said Uncle was alive, not with the Italians or the Partisans but that he had joined an Ustashi unit hiding in the small bay below Marjan. And, they added, the unit would raid our house one day and shoot all of us because someone can't be a member of the Ustashi unless the whole family are Ustashi. You could hear all kinds of things in those years. Your aunt wanted to join the Partisans herself, hoping it would help her find her husband at one of the fronts. You weren't sure what kept her from heading up into the mountain forests. Your mother once said, 'She just talks like that; how could she leave the comfort of her own bed.' Surprisingly, your father, didn't join the Partisans. He thought somehow that they wouldn't take him because his left leg was shorter than his right. He wouldn't be able to run and attack like the others. Was the truth that he was afraid? That's how it seems to me. After all, even soldiers who get injured in battle rarely return from war. They want to serve their army and their fatherland to the end. How could the two-centimeter difference he was born with in his legs keep your father from firing in an ambush? Your father was destined to end in failure; here he was, a fisherman left behind without fish and without a voice in his house. It's not clear to me how you survived those war years with no income, with nothing. That's what you wanted to talk about least of all. 'Ah, Nedi, it was war,' you'd say repeatedly. Still, you and your aunt could have sewn expensive dresses and blouses for all the women connected to the Italian and German officers rather than sewing for the partisans for free, but you put your conscience ahead of your earnings.

Whenever I asked Granddad Carlo what it was like when he was a soldier in the army, he waved his hand and fell silent at the mere thought of anything connected with that period of his life. He was not like the grandfathers in the movies who take their children on their knee and tell them about the things they witnessed in the war. With each of Granddad's stories—because I heard them so rarely—I felt like I was becoming reacquainted with him.

AH NEDI, what do you want with war stories? Are there so few of them? They go on and on, you can't see their beginning or their end, but when you talk about them, you could simply sum them up in three sentences and not be wrong. Three years in three sentences. God damn those years! It was like I was in prison from '41 to '43. I was stuck at home and couldn't go anywhere. I'd lost nearly all contact with my friends. My aunt and I sewed for days on end, and sometimes when Yuri was at our place, we begged him to sing us Russian songs, and when he finished, he'd say: 'Come on now, Krsto, sing one of your songs,' but Krsto didn't want to hear about it. He never sang a song again. The dangling little finger on his left hand was a constant reminder of that terrible day in the Bačvice camp. It's not like I was bored those years; it's never boring in war time, you never know what or when something is going to happen to you, and during each air attack, we all ran to the cellar, except Papa. He absolutely refused to hide even if his life depended on it. He just stayed put, most often at the kitchen table, leafing through an old edition of the 'New Times' that Mama hadn't yet burned in the oven. We had no present, just air raids, and every thought was about hunger, poverty, and misery, but who wanted to think about such things? That's why we looked to the past, and whenever we had several hours of peace and quiet in the city, I wanted most of all for Mama and Papa to tell me about things that happened in their lives that I hadn't been part of. I learned some interesting things from Papa that I'd never heard from anyone else. For example, when he was still a young boy, one April around 1910, people in Split were saying that the end of the world would come on May 18. Halley's comet was going to hit the Earth and that would be the end, there would be nothing left on the planet. People talked so much about it that an unbelievable atmosphere took over the city: some people spent the last days of their lives cut loose, singing, making merry, selling everything they had for a piece of meat and a bottle of wine, and unbridled moans of passion could be heard at night from the windows of Split. There were others who were scared to death by the approaching evil and they sobbed and wailed, without even going out of their houses, hugging each other for the last time, and treating their children with extra kindness, even forgiving their mischievousness, for which before they would have been harshly punished. The day arrived: 18 May 1910. The whole city poured onto the Riva. It was like a holiday. Everyone stood there all night, waiting for the end of the world. They were dressed in their finest, hair done, washed, spiffed-up, the children dressed in their holiday clothes, as if for a christening, the women with beautiful gold jewelry around their necks, bedecked and perfumed. It looked like a large festive gathering on some big day or the celebration of the arrival of an important personage. It was a happy mood, not gloomy or solemn; it was as if everyone would meet again in heaven when the world collapsed. They stood there on the Riva, celebrating until the wee hours, but the end of the world didn't come. 'I was a little disappointed,' Papa told me. 'How could someone play around with people like that?' My mother's most vivid memory was the year 1927, when I was four years old before Krsto was born. They'd left me with Grandma, Granddad, and my uncle, who was still a bachelor, and she went out with Papa for a promenade on the Corso and along the Riva. 'Weren't you uncomfortable promenading on the Corso now that you were a married woman? With a child at home no less?' I once asked her. 'I didn't think about it like that,' she answered. I tried again: 'I mean, didn't other people judge you? Didn't they smirk at you and Papa traipsing along the Corso? It should have been Uncle out on the Corso, not you—he wasn't married. I don't know, I'm just asking, even though I think married women need to go out walking with their husbands and not just stay home wiping baby bums.' 'Maybe we shouldn't have been out walking the Corso, but that 1927 was special. There had never been so many people on the Riva. Where had all those people, nearly all young people, come from? Was it because it was hot, but not too hot? Or because there weren't any mosquitos like in past years? I don't know, but young and old were out on the Corso, everyone, that is, except your uncle. He was always a strange one. I don't know how he found your aunt since he never left the house. But look how he turned out—he's off with the Partisans or wherever he is, while your father is the one who turned into a real home-body.' 'So what did you do on the Corso? Just stroll?' 'Yes, but what a stroll it was, you can't imagine! There was such a crowd of people that we were bumping into one another, jostling each other with our elbows and stepping on each other's toes. Every so often someone would fall down and panic would set in, and we'd all get pushed aside. In fact, it was dangerous walking like that, squeezed next to each other like sardines, but outdoors. Then, one evening the municipal guards showed up and began to organize things. Literally, they lined us up in four columns, two by two: two columns pointed to the east, two columns to the west. And from that day on that's how we had to walk on the Corso. There were notices posted on storefronts. *Walking is permitted only two by two, in two columns.* Two going one way, two the other. And in the middle of everything, there were guards walking around with bayonets warning anyone who stepped out of line. It was like we were in a parade. The hustle and bustle died down. We walked in silence, holding on to our partner's arm. No one spoke aloud, or laughed, or teased one another. The young boys who had previously walked in groups on the Corso were now spread out, two-by-two, more like soldiers than bachelors wanting to tease their girl in the crowd. I won't even mention the girls who used to walk together in groups with flushed cheeks, eyes sparkling. Now they didn't laugh, or sing, or blush in embarrassment. They hurried along. But the Corso was supposed to be a slow promenade. It was supposed to be relaxing. Your father and I walked a few more days, and then that was it. The two-columned walking bored us. But I can't forget it because nothing like that had happened in Split before or since. There was no longer a Corso there, except when your brother's Italians were out walking.' That's what she always called them, 'your brother's,' as if they were Krsto's friends, which, in fact they had been, until that incident with the soldier who broke Krsto's left pinky.

But I also still remember one of the saddest things that happened, if one can even call it that given the Fascists' occupation of Split, and that was when the statue of Gregory of Nin was removed from the peristyle in Diocletian's palace around November of '41, when Krsto and Yuri were still going to sing for the Italian occupiers. The statue, which is now in front of the Golden Gates, had originally been placed in our Split peristyle by its sculptor, Ivan Meštrović. It had been the source of my six-year-old self's civic pride. How had they managed to bring it by train? Did they load it in a freight car? I remember that event like in a fog—all of us children running along the rails to greet him. And now, the Italian soldiers had come marching along 'Marmontova Street' which—without asking any of us locals—they had rechristened 'Via Mussolini,' dismantled Gregory of Nin, and carried him off somewhere while we girls cried over him as if he had been our boyfriend, not a statue of a medieval bishop.

November 1942, Split

BETWEEN 1941 TO 1943, Grandma did not see Charlotte a single time. Despite Split's small size, it was difficult to simply run into someone during wartime. Charlotte didn't come even once to their house. There was no reason to, though she might have because of the French fashion catalogue and patterns she'd sent through Krsto. My Grandma often thought of Charlotte, but she wasn't brave enough to run to their house in the Dobri neighbourhood, even though she knew that her French teacher would have been extremely glad to see her after a whole year had passed since the high school closed. Grandma told me she often imagined Charlotte, smiling, beautiful, well-dressed, and happy. She couldn't imagine her any other way. In her young mind, every woman who would move to another country for love must be a woman who was happy and loved. It wasn't clear whether Krsto ever passed by Charlotte's, but he never mentioned her again and didn't bring anything to my Grandma from her. But sometime around the end of '42, he mentioned in passing: 'Do you remember that French woman? She had a baby!' That's all he said. Grandma was startled when she heard the news, as was their mother, who of course added, 'Who gives birth in wartime? Leave it to the French!' 'Was it a boy or a girl?' 'I don't know, I didn't ask,' said Krsto. But Grandma ran straight upstairs to her aunt and asked, 'Can you show me how to make a little baby dress?' They sat right down at the sewing machine and, from the scraps of fabric thrown to the bottom of the sewing machine cabinet, made a marvelous little multi-coloured dress, decorated in squares and triangles—what I'd call a cubist design. It was so small and sweet that Grandma couldn't resist trying it on the only doll they had at home, a plastic, pink doll used for decoration; it was dressed in a wedding dress and veil, and the clear bag protecting it was no longer transparent but covered in dust. No one had ever dared play with the doll with its googly eyes and pale red lips, or even remove it from its bag; it had just stood in the kitchen cupboard ever since the day Grandma's mother brought it home from Rijeka as part of her trousseau. But now Grandma couldn't resist. She climbed up on a chair, pulled it down, undressed it, wiped off the dust, and dressed it in the little dress for Charlotte's newborn. It's interesting that she didn't doubt, not even for a second, that the baby was a girl. Everything was so pretty—the doll in its little dress, the little dress on the doll. She wrapped the dress in a sheet of newspaper, thrust it into Krsto's hand and said, 'Take this to Miss Charlotte. Tell her it's from Non-Oui, tell her just like that.' Krsto waited for the fighting in the west side of the city to die down, then he ran, sometimes almost crawling hunched close to the ground, to bring the small present to Charlotte. He handed it through the bars of the basement window where Charlotte, a Parisian who had lived near Montmartre, with a balcony nearly as big as a house, had now been living all these years with her in-laws in two basement rooms with insufficient light for the Split journals that she most likely didn't even write for any longer. 'Love, now that's what love is,' Grandma Neda would repeat. Krsto came back holding a red cap—a woman's velvet beret with a small silk tassel, a greeting from Charlotte for Grandma. 'It's a boy, not a girl,' he said.

NONNA, you wore that cap September 8, 1943, the day Italy's capitulation was announced on the radio. Towards evening everybody went out on the Riva and every single person was wearing some piece of red cloth: the girls and women put a red bow in their hair or pinned one to their chest, and the boys and the men slipped a red kerchief into their buttonholes or held a piece of red cloth or a red banner in their hands. It looked like a painting! But on that warm September of '43 you were the only one wearing a red hat, a beret—something more suited for winter. Why didn't you put a red ribbon in your hair? What compelled you to grab Charlotte's beret and put it on? You wore a summer dress, the most beautiful one, which you had saved for that moment when 'the war would be over,' the one you'd sewn with your aunt back in '42. Every eye turned your way to see what was on your head, everyone looked with a touch of wonder, but also a secret understanding, as if acknowledging that everything was allowed to celebrate victory, even the wearing of a winter cap at the beginning of September. Krsto and Yuri ran with the other children through the mass of people, shouting at the top of their lungs, 'Free Dalmatia! Free Dalmatia!,' as they handed out the first edition of the newspaper published in Split. When they went past you and your girlfriends, whom you hadn't seen for an eternity, Yuri burst out laughing and shouted! 'A red cap? Red, just like Little Red Riding Hood!' But you weren't embarrassed, were you? When I think about it, I don't think you were a shy person, though you often ended up in situations where you couldn't help behaving shyly. I read that this is particularly true of people who move to a new place and become unsure of themselves. They lose their self-confidence and other people who have lived their whole lives in the same place without changing locations, think it's their shyness.

AH, NEDI, what a day that was! You were forever asking me what it was like during the war, and it was hard for me to tell you about it, and harder still for your Granddad, but the day I can tell you about was our day of victory. On the 8th of September, people began to disarm the soldiers on the side of the city in front of the Hotel Park where the Italian headquarters had been. Now, don't go imagining that this was so simple, that you just go up to someone, and just take everything they have and that's it. We stood a bit off to the side, watching them filled with a sense of our victory, looking at them rather impertinently for girls. I was twenty years old. Can you imagine? I was embarrassed in front of men; many years had gone by since my first boyfriend. After my first and, at that time, my last love, which I'll tell you about someday, I didn't really know exactly what a man, a young man, looked like. The Italian soldiers were young men, my age, or a bit older, and they were all so handsome, so young, so vibrant. And now—prisoners of war. The local people took their weapons, their caps, even their handkerchiefs, whether they were snotty or not, from their pockets, and their wallets. Some of them protested. One soldier shouted as loud as he could, 'That's a photo of my girlfriend!' but the man who took his wallet, a friend of my father's, also a fisherman, simply yanked the photo from his pocket and tore it to pieces right before the soldier's eyes. I began to hate old Simo right then and there. How could he do that? The soldier began yelling and swearing in Italian, probably also fuming that Italy had capitulated. But some of the men gave up their arms and joined the celebration with us. There was complete chaos, joy, and madness. At one point, I caught myself tossing the beret with one hand then waiting to catch it with the same hand. Me, who people considered a quiet girl!

But then maybe I wasn't. Maybe it was simply the war that had made me quiet and stand-offish; I was cooped up at home, a prisoner of the war. That day when Italy capitulated and we were all on the Riva, Papa stayed home, claiming he didn't feel well. His head hurt and he felt dizzy. But he said we should go and not worry about him. When we returned, he was sleeping. We thought he was better. That's why I went back out into town, with the beret once again on my head. I could not have enjoyed the city more than at this moment, after Italy's capitulation. It had been almost three years that I hadn't seen the city, just hanging around Auntie's room or the basement, with almost no contact with my friends and no classes. When my friends and I saw each other on the Riva, we marveled at how each of us had grown, shot up, become beautiful. Can a person become more beautiful in wartime? Youth charts its own course, passes through its own stages. Nearly all of us were twenty years old, still unmarried, almost never even touched by a man's hand. Several had even gone off and joined the Partisans. That evening and the following two, those of us who had remained in Split just walked and walked. It's not that we weren't afraid–there were Italian soldiers who'd been disarmed wandering the city with almost nothing, smoking their last cigarettes, cigarettes that had most likely been hidden in their underwear, and sharing a bottle. At the harbour I noticed a group of people with a red cross on their sleeves doling out food—bowls of soup—and the soldiers who weren't wandering about just sat there and watched from a distance. 'They're waiting for the Red Cross ship to take them to Italy,' people whispered along the Riva. These were the soldiers who had decided to go home and continue being what they had been: Fascists. 'Fascists!' shouted Yulia as we passed them. I pinched her elbow. But the next moment I heard myself shouting, first in a trembling voice, and then more forcefully, 'Fascists! Fascists!' One of them turned and shouted to me, 'Hey there Little Red Riding Hood, the wolf is soon going to gobble you up!' but I heard another voice behind me answering, 'It should gobble you up, not her!' 'What did they say?' I asked Yulia who knew Italian well. I didn't turn around to see who was trying to defend me.

THE DAY THAT ITALY CAPITULATED and Grandma went out to the Riva wearing her red hat, a red flag was unfurled on Marjan, and all those gathered on the Riva began to sing the patriotic song 'Hey, Slavs.' Once the Italian soldiers had been disarmed, people ran through the Italian warehouses and stores, carrying off everything they could find: flour, oil, sugar, everything. Amidst the tumult on the square, Grandma caught sight of Charlotte, whom she hadn't seen since '41. She was holding her son, Marcel, in her arms. He was one year old, dressed in blue pants and, over them, the little dress that my Grandma and her aunt had sewn because Grandma was convinced Charlotte had had a girl. 'A woman that beautiful,' thought Grandma, 'can only give birth to a girl.' Charlotte was even more lovely and elegant, but she had dark circles under her eyes. The French teacher tenderly held her elbow. My Grandma instinctively ran towards them. When Charlotte saw her wearing the red beret she'd sent with Krsto, she hugged her with her free hand and at that moment Grandma and Marcel, the twenty-year-old woman and the one-year-old little boy, touched cheeks. Grandma would say to me, 'I will never forget that touch of Marcel's little face. And my embarrassment over the little dress. Even though he was wearing it like a tunic over his pants. Ah, French fashion! And there I was wearing the beret his mother had given me.' I think that's how people become the closest in life, through these small and insignificant moments of total connection with another. 'I would have done everything for Marcel, even given my life,' Grandma told me, pursing her lips, both of us with the same thought: 'What did you do?' Charlotte began speaking to her in Croatian, since during those few years Charlotte had mastered the language and spoke in the Split dialect with a French accent. Marcel spoke baby talk with both Croatian and French sounds. It was clear that my Grandma was very dear to Charlotte, and several times she joked with her, 'Ne-da, that's who you are, right? Non-Oui, Non-Oui.' But Grandma Neda, Non-Oui—which I also called her, especially when I came home from school and I would find her sitting lightly sun-burned, and motionless on the garden swing—just blushed, a desire suddenly coming to life inside her for her own child, and for a man all hers, someone who would love her the way my French teacher had fallen in love with Charlotte when she came to Split on board that ship in 1939.

1938, Split

BUT NONNA NON-OUI, you already knew what love was. Remember? You told me about your first love, about Krunoslav, the boy with the difficult name but the easy-going spirit? You were fifteen and he was seventeen. It was your first year in the girls' high school and his third year in the boys'. You met in the literary club at his school, which you had learned about from your French teacher because he thought you were good at recitation. He said that even though you didn't write poetry yourself, it might still be good to go and get acquainted with young, promising poets. You had gotten a math assignment back that day with a C- and you were worried how you would tell your father, not to mention your mother, so you went to the literary club in the basement of the school across town. There were mostly boys there, plus two other girls besides you. You noticed him immediately: tall, slender, in a blue knit sweater, a scarf around his neck, something you'd never seen any other boy wear. His hair was cut short at the top, but around his eyes it fell in thick curls, honey-blond hair that sparkled like gold in the light. He came right up to you, which was surprising in those pre-war years of youthful—almost childish—bashfulness, and he asked whether you wrote poetry. You shook your head, then asked him whether he did well in math because you didn't understand the errors you'd made on your C- assignment. He sat down beside you, and together you worked through the math problems at the literary club. Then, after explaining everything he knew, he got up and read aloud two poems that took your breath away. You left with a completely new feeling in your chest, as if your body had grown a new internal organ, one for him alone, for that one and only Krunoslav.

Ah, Nedi, a new organ grew inside me again when I gave birth to your uncle Mario. First love, an organ for love. First child, a new organ for children. And when your Granddad died, an organ inside me died, something I didn't even know I'd had. The body is made up of these organs of the spirit, Nedi. Until that moment, I didn't know you could grow a new one, one completely different, one that could either hurt or strengthen your body as well as your soul. That's how it was when I met Krunoslav. We saw each other every Wednesday at the club in his school. At home, I told my parents I had to go because we also worked on math problems there. After the third meeting, he invited me to take a walk with him and Sonja, a student who was older than me, who also went to my school but with whom I spoke for the first time at the club. Sonja said, 'I don't have time!' and I looked at her pleadingly because I didn't want to go alone with him. That wasn't proper. Even though it was already 1938 and Split was a pretty modern town where the winds seemed to gust with a European air, a young woman still didn't go out so easily on a date with a young man. 'Go alone, that's what he wants,' Sonja whispered to me, as if we were good friends, when, in fact, it was the first time we'd had a conversation. 'Please!' I begged her. We went together to Bačvice, sat by the sea, and tossed pebbles. We were silent, thinking our own thoughts. Sonja lived nearby, and she set off for home alone, but Krunoslav accompanied me as far as the Riva. 'I had an extremely lovely afternoon,' he said. At the next meeting of the club, he asked me, 'Would you like to get together on Friday? At the bench behind the theater?' I just nodded. I couldn't find my voice. I was falling deeper and deeper in love with him. I felt the love organ growing inside my body, and it was eclipsing all the others, or maybe it was giving them new life, I don't know. But that Friday, I was utterly in love by the time I arrived, dressed in a red skirt and a black silk blouse. I had put a red flower in my hair. You're laughing? Of course, today it seems silly, but at the time it felt to me like the most serious thing in the world. We sat for a few minutes, without saying a word, then we stood and set off on a walk. He suggested we go to Diocletian's palace, down to the underground floors. There in the damp and dark rooms he hugged me and said, 'You know, you're very intelligent.' 'Intelligent?' I didn't know that someone would tell a girl that she was intelligent on their first romantic date. They'd usually say she was pretty, gorgeous, magical—that's what I'd heard anyway from Yulia, who understood these things. But Krunoslav was like that. I blushed and didn't say a word. I just lowered my head to his chest, and we stood like that a whole eternity. Later we kissed. And we did not stop kissing. When I got home, I felt like my lips were swollen and that everyone would notice. I went right to bed, but Krsto kept playing for another whole hour with a marble or something like that, and it would hit the corner of the room again and again. My heart was banging in my head, and I thought my face would burst and all that would be left would be my mouth, hot and swollen, and I would never again be able to kiss Krunoslav with that mouth.

HIS MOUTH MUST HAVE BEEN THE SAME. Whenever they met, my Grandma and Krunoslav would mainly just kiss in silence. Then, at the end of each meeting Krunoslav would recite his poems to her. She didn't write poems, even though she could recite foreign ones, mostly poems in French that her teacher insisted they learn by heart; she just listened and devoured his. One day he suggested they write a poem together, or, more precisely, they should compose it, but not write it down. They began. He would compose a line or two, then she would, until they had a whole poem. That evening Grandma lit a candle by her bedside and wrote the poem from memory in her mathematics notebook. The experience had been so intense that she remembered every word. Krunoslav was grateful that she had written it down because by the time he got home, he had already forgotten it. He said he'd been able to remember his lines, but not hers; he'd never been able to recite anyone else's poems but his own. It was the only poem they wrote together. Their romantic connection lasted only half a year. Her love grew, but his seemed to stand in place, is how Grandma described it to me. She usually wanted them to be alone, while he more frequently took her to hang out with his friends. None of them had a girlfriend, so sometimes Sonja went out with them, but she didn't fall in love with any of his friends. When Krunoslav and my Grandma were kissing, his friends would generally get bored, hop in place, chew on blades of grass, and could barely wait to continue along some narrow alleyway in the city. Grandma whispered to me that she was still a virgin, and that besides petting, him touching her breasts, and them stroking between each other's legs, nothing serious had happened with Krunoslav. She told him she wanted to lose her virginity on her wedding night, because that was how she'd been raised. He just kept silent and kissed her more passionately. Then, a month came when he kissed her more lightly and less often. He began to recite poems in which he lamented how everything must end, how one couldn't fight against oneself, and how one day she would understand him. Grandma could still remember the day when, before she left the house, her mother made amazing cookies from flour and water, without sugar because there wasn't any, but inside she'd tucked a dab of fig jam. Grandma didn't try them because they were still hot, but she told herself she'd have at least one when she got back from her meeting with Krunoslav. And she set off. Of course, no one in the household knew she was meeting a boy; it was especially important that Krsto not find out. Krunoslav arrived for their date pale, with dark circles under his eyes. He didn't even kiss her. He just handed her a bunch of poems in two piles tied with string. He began quietly and wearily to sing a song about autumn that arrived and carried away their love like a swallow. Then he just turned and left. That was the end.

Grandma barely dragged herself home, the bundle of poems in her hand. It didn't even occur to her to taste the cookies. She lay down and trembled all night from cold and tears. This was the first great calamity in her life. The greatest tragedy. The greatest pain. The greatest loss. Although this was happening for the first time in her life, she already knew there could be nothing worse than this.

'HOW IS THAT POSSIBLE, NONNA? Just imagine if one of your children had died. Or when Granddad died, wasn't that as big a misfortune? I remember you cried for days, and once you even fell unconscious. You weren't as sad when your father died?' 'I don't know,' she said to me whenever I asked. 'I mean, really, what if Papà died or Uncle Mario or Uncle Luca? Or me?' I would ask, not believing her firm conviction that when she was only fifteen years old, after her first romantic relationship, she would feel that that break-up was the greatest tragedy of her life. And no matter what happened after that, including, apparently, the death of Granddad Carlo, whom she truly loved, it could not compare with that loss from back before the war. 'There was another thing that mattered to me. Krunoslav couldn't die before me. First me, then him. Not the other way around.' 'But Nonna, you haven't seen him for nearly fifty years! How can you talk like that? Besides, who knows what happened to him after all these years? Who knows where he is or whether he's even alive! Or if he even remembers you.' I had to add that because it's not like I didn't care that all of us closest to her meant less than some Krunoslav or other, whom she loved as a young girl, a child really. 'But I loved him forever. I never stopped loving him, though that love changed when I met your grandfather. I fell in love with him but in a different way. I loved Krunoslav as something that was my own and that I preserved within me, like a body part that I don't want to ever give up or have removed, even if it rotted and I could die from it.' 'Good Lord, Nonna!'

Only a few years later she learned that Krunoslav had moved to England with his uncle even before the war and then, years later, during her first trip to Split, she learned that he had never returned and, to the shame of his uncle, who brought him there and his poor mother left alone in Split, he didn't take a wife after the war in England, but lived with a man, an Englishman. They lived together like man and wife, and he did those things with him that should only be done with a woman. That's what Sonja said to her years later, when they met in the church by the market at the memorial mass that was held for the dead who were exhumed from the medieval cemetery in Sustipan. When they caught sight of one another, Sonja stayed behind and led my Grandma outside to the front of the church and quickly told her everything she'd heard about Krunoslav. 'That's everything you wanted to know, right?' 'Did he become a poet?' Grandma asked right away, and when Sonja shrugged her shoulders, Grandma went back into the church, but she didn't pray for the soul of her father, exhumed and reburied, or for anyone else. All she saw before her was Krunoslav kissing a man in far-off England.

AH NEDI, even today my heart pounds when I think about him. He must still be alive because he sometimes appears in my dreams. The dead are never in my dreams. Your Granddad, for example, never appears, though I want to see him so much. But what would he say to me? After all, he was silent for a full two years before he died, so he's not going to start talking now that he's dead. But Krunoslav gets in touch in my dreams and tells me things. The last time I dreamt that I had a letter from him in which he wrote: 'Do you know what's the most important thing in your life? You must know.' And before that I had a dream where we're lying together, God forgive me, naked, on the ground in some apartment of his, and Sonja leaps into the bedroom right up onto the bed dressed in a wedding gown, and she tries to throw the bridal bouquet a few times, but it keeps landing at her feet rather than behind her. Krunoslav and I are lying there naked, embracing, just as young as we had been. I didn't want to wake from the dream. I didn't want to wake into the present. It's strange, isn't it? Such loves exist, Nedi, they do. Or love like I had with your Granddad, different, but long and deep. I'm so sorry you still haven't experienced anything like this. In my time you'd already be an old maid, my girl. How is it that you have never liked a single young man! How is it possible? But I see that your girl friends are not busy worrying about those things either. Then there's Margherita, who brings home that older man. What is with you children? You'll get old and you'll have no memories. And even if you do, you'll have no one you can tell them to. Will you give birth in your old age?

YOU'RE RIGHT, Nonna, I don't know what love is. I'm twenty-six but still don't know what it means to make love with someone you love. I only know meaningless sex, most often with myself, if I don't count sleeping with men at drunken parties on the bay. And it's not for religious or romantic reasons, like you had, for example when you were with Krunoslav but planned to lose your virginity on your wedding night. I'm not a virgin, but I can't even remember when it happened and with whom—that's what it's like when a person's drunk and under the influence of various pills dropped into one's beer. I don't know what war is either. I haven't felt its weight on my own back. I also don't know what it means to move, I've lived my whole life in this house where you came from Split because of Granddad; my life is like my peers in just about every detail, except one: their grandparents are Italians, Sicilians, most often, but I have you, a woman from Split, a foreigner, a newcomer. That's all that distinguishes my life from theirs, but that's no small thing. I don't think anything else will set me apart. I don't feel any desire to be with someone. I can't imagine leaving this house, not to mention this country—even though I want to travel, you know that yourself. I want to travel, move around, allow myself everything I can, but then come home. In some way, Mamma and Papà and I all depend on one another. But not Margherita. Margherita will leave home soon; she told me that herself. As soon as her boyfriend divorces his wife and brings her to his place. That's what she thinks, but I think she's only deceiving herself. After all, in a small town like ours, is it really possible for someone to get divorced and start afresh? In our small narrow streets, especially along the seacoast, it's impossible not to keep running into a former lover. Not to mention the children. For the children it's totally delightful to run into their father somewhere nearly every day, but for the new wife? The new couple? I don't think Margherita has the strength to endure it. She's better off the way things are now: she sees Pietro when he has time to meet, or when his wife is off in Palermo at her parents with the children. Then Margherita packs up all her sexiest clothes and off she goes to his place, and when she comes back, I think she's three kilos lighter; her eyes are shining, she's got a smooth tan, she's all smiles and full of energy. 'Sex does the trick.' That's what you once whispered to me when you saw me staring at her, surprised by her energy. She's been seeing Pietro for several years now, almost since she was still a child. How did no one suspect that she, such a young woman, was seeing a married man? People say his wife is a bit absent-minded, and apparently in her free time paints flowers, stars, moons, and still-lifes. It seems that in her imagination she also knows how to depict marital bliss really well. Yet, this evening Margherita will stay home while Pietro celebrates New Year's with his family. What kind of love is that? A double one? I don't have the strength for one, let alone two. This evening we'll hang around down at the bay with the Irish tourists we met today in 'Rio bar,' and then anything and everything could happen.

Anything and everything, but I wouldn't think of ever moving away from this house. To think I would fill my suitcase with everything I own to go off and live someplace else. It was even hard for me to move into your room two weeks ago, right after you died, but I had to, not just for Margherita, so Pietro could occasionally come to our house, to her room, that is, but also so I could be closer to you, feel the traces of your steps on the parquet floor and be able for the hundredth time to open your closets, where I didn't let Mamma throw away any of your clothes and other things. I tucked my stuff in the far nook by the door, where you kept your suitcase from Split. Now the suitcase languishes under the bed, so I even have the suitcase if I ever want to move somewhere, I mean, forever. Like you did. But ever since I was little, you always taught me: 'Ah, Nedi, I hope in your life you never have to move away somewhere. Stay where you are. You don't know what it means to settle somewhere else. If someone loves you so much, let him move where you are.' And that stuck not only in my mind, but in my soul, in the very pores of my skin. That's why I decided to stay here, in this house. And, you know, I work in the largest bookstore in Palermo and travel forty kilometers by bus in each direction every day. It would make the most sense for me to rent an apartment and walk to work. But I can't imagine coming home and being met by an empty room without the smell of dinner and without sounds, the everyday sounds, the sounds of people. If I had my own family, that is, a husband and children, that would make sense, it would be normal. But I don't and what's worse, or better, depending on how you look at it, I don't want to have them. Things are fine for me the way they are, although sometimes when I walk along the shore with Mamma and Papà, the tourists give me an odd look, some even take photos of me. But what are they so struck by? I also see tourists during the summer who come with their families: husband, wife, and a grown son, on the beach taking turns with the sunscreen lotion, sitting down for some pizza or spaghetti somewhere and talking in a friendly way, agreeing on what to order, the mother laughs at her son's smart jokes, the father makes a toast with him, they take selfies and most likely post them on Facebook, and then they like each other's photos. An ideal family, but the son is around twenty-seven or twenty-eight. Wouldn't it be more ideal if he were sitting at the table with a girlfriend or a wife and child? For a woman, they say it's even more important. Once I saw a young married couple together with an older woman, most likely the mother or mother-in-law dressed in an awful, loud, gold bathing suit. 'Is that how they sleep?' I wondered. When I look at them and at myself, sometimes I am seized by a terrible fear that in the end, I'll be left completely alone, childless, with no one in the world, and at other times I'm seized with longing for a family, but still, that's all so remote for me. It's the same with my friends. I don't know what happened to my generation. It seems the same thing is happening everywhere, but especially in developed countries. Take my friends, for example, Mira's the only one with a boyfriend. They go out two or three times a week, and that's it. Sarah got pregnant by her boyfriend Pavel, but they have no plans to get married, and she doesn't think that this will cause them to. Plus, she has no idea where or how they would live. She doesn't want to give up her childhood room to go live with Pavel, who has two younger brothers plus a grandfather in a wheelchair. The others are also like me. They live at home with their parents, and when we go out together, we're all struck by the fact that we talk more about our mothers and fathers, what they bought us for our birthdays, or how we went out to eat yesterday at *Dorotea*, asking each other through our laughter, 'Who did you go with?' 'With Mamma and Papà,' 'What about you?' 'Same with me.' 'Was Margherita there?' 'No, Pietro was with her.' 'Does his wife know?' 'Apparently, she knows, but it's more convenient for her not to know.' And for us, we're closer to our parents than our friends. It's strange that it doesn't bother any of us that our parents are so present in our lives, it's even taken for granted. I don't know whether we're sick or whether that's just what the world is like. Or is it our parents' fault we're like this?

But I am not important, what interests me is the story of my Grandma Nedjeljka. Ever since she died, not a day has gone when I haven't wanted to speak with her. Her life left more memories than three of my lives ever could, and I have no one to pass them on to anyway.

September 1943, Split

AH, NEDI, I pretty much never went home those few days following Italy's surrender. I was out the whole time with my friends on the Riva. There were fewer Italian soldiers on shore, but there were still some. There hadn't been just a few in Split. There had been more than a thousand! Most had already sailed back on special ships that Italy had sent. Others fled on whatever ship they could find in the harbour, and it wasn't unusual for us to find a drowned body washed up on shore. Others left on the Red Cross ships, gazing one last time towards the country where they had arrived as enemies and departed as enemies. The locals, especially us young people, shouted after them: 'Hey, you Fascists! Beat it! Go home!' The children threw stones and shot at them with slingshots. The Partisans tried to maintain some sort of order. There were reports that the soldiers who decided to stay behind and become Partisans had already formed their own battalion. This was, in fact, the first Italian anti-fascist battalion, the Garibaldi, which was founded just ten days after the surrender. It was made up of three hundred and fifty former Italian soldiers, most of them carabinieri.

But out on the Riva, you couldn't tell at first glance which soldiers were staying, and which ones were leaving. Some were probably still thinking about what to do. It's not easy to change your point of view just like that, especially your political view. Up to now you've been a fascist, so how can you become an anti-fascist? True, Italy had surrendered, but not everyone thinks the same way as their leader or the state. It was later that I understood that for a solder the most important thing is, in fact, simply to go home. Unless the person is a real fighter, in his blood; of course, there are some like that. The Italian soldiers were young like us, okay, maybe a few years older, but to us, to us girls, they all looked young and handsome. When had we seen so many young men in one place in our whole lives? While we were going to school, we'd gone separately, the boys to the boys' high school, and the girls to the girls' high school. Before the war we'd still been too young to meet young men on the Corso, though each of us had, in one way or another, experienced our first love. And nearly all those had an unhappy ending. The boyfriends of the older girls in the city were now mostly away with the Partisans and they would feel sad if there were no one waiting for them if, in the meantime, their girls fell in love with others, but my Krunoslav was in England, far from my eyes and heart. I thought of him like a dead man but one who couldn't die before me. It was a strange feeling, one I always wanted to block out with someone else, to cover over, and forget. Maybe that's why I was so bubbly when my girlfriends and I walked on the Riva and looked at the soldiers a bit too impertinently for our gender and age. 'Fascists!' we would shout at them in unison. They gave as good as they got. Some made hand gestures to show how big our breasts were, others raised their middle finger, but no one stopped to molest us physically. They were too tired of life to do anything like that.

SO NONNA, how did you manage to meet Carlo just then?

I would ask you that question at least once a month while you sat on the swing in the garden. You'd sit there without swinging, and I would lie on the grass near your dangling feet and ask you to tell me again how you met. I've always been fascinated by how two people can be together and remain together just because they met at the right place at the right time. What does it mean 'to be in the right place at the right time?' Are all encounters in life like that? Or is it sometimes the case that you're in the wrong place at the right time? Or the right place at the wrong time? That's when the worst encounters in life take place I think. 'Take the Italians, for example, they were in the wrong place at the right time. In Split, far from home, that is, and then Italy surrenders.' That's the example you gave me, remember? Or your Papa was in the wrong place at the wrong time, and that's why he was shot by that random Italian soldier. Or when Margherita met Pietro, she was in the right place, at a house party in our little town, but at the wrong time—she got there just five minutes before he left, and bingo! They meet at the door, and he comes back in and that was the end of that, or rather the beginning of their relationship, even though he had a wife and children at home. That's how you explained variations in time and place. But I was most interested in you and Granddad. After all, wasn't he also one of the soldiers left in the wrong place at the right time? 'No,' you'd insist, 'your Granddad was in my right time and in my right place.' In fact, it's only your brother, no matter how much you don't like him, that you had to thank that Carlo was there right then. Your brother usually ran away when he saw you with your girlfriends. He spent most of his time with Yuri, but Yuri, who was 'totally Russian school,' you'd say with a smile, would always come up and say hello, or at least tease you, like when he called you *Little Red Riding Hood*. Cheerful, blond, blue-eyed, already as tall as you and your girlfriends, he was really a nice young man. Only it was a pity, you always added, that he was friends with Krsto. It's normal for sisters to say that it's too bad that their brothers' friends are good-for-nothings, but you said about Yuri that it was too bad he was a friend of your brother's. That day, as you passed by the soldiers with your friends, flirtatious in the dresses you now wore with more flair than ever, you watched Yuri and Krsto take aim with a slingshot at one of the soldiers sitting at the edge of the harbour, evidently waiting for a rescue ship from Italy. He clapped his hands over his eyes, but the shot struck his ear and blood poured out. The soldier had nothing on him but his small, military pack, which was empty. He didn't even have a handkerchief. 'Hey, should we sing you some Sicilian songs now? Would you like that?' Yuri shouted in Croatian with the marked Russian accent he got from his father, but your brother began singing 'Marjane, Marjane.' The soldiers chased after them, fists raised, but they didn't dare take a swing at them. Why not? Who were they afraid of? The people around them? The men who were crowded around the harbour looked like insects, immobile so you couldn't tell if they were dead or alive. That's how you could take advantage of them. What was it that bubbled to the surface just then inside of you and your friends? It was less the blood on the soldier's ear, than the fact that he suddenly pulled his hands away from his eyes. And that movement revealed something special. 'What eyes! I had never seen such big eyes in my life.' It's too bad Uncle Mario was the only one to inherit them. There was something feminine about those eyes; they were like an actress's, the eyes of film stars, eyes like Sophia Loren, Elizabeth Taylor, or Grace Kelly. Nonna, as soon as you saw those eyes of his, you were bewitched. You pulled your handkerchief from your bag and went over to wipe his ear. But what was most astonishing was that first you turned to Krsto, grabbed him by the ear, and spun him in a circle. Where did a twenty-year old girl get such strength? From love? Yuri couldn't help laughing. Krsto wanted to grab your hand and bite your wrist like he always did, but you just pushed him away, or maybe one of your friends shoved him off, while you, with your small white handkerchief, bandaged the soldier's ear, looking, or more precisely, staring into his enormous eyes. And he looked into yours, though neither of you said a word. And that was that. Is that what it means to be in the right place at the right time? Or is it only later that a person understands that it was then and there?

AH, NEDI, those weren't eyes! They were the entire Adriatic Sea scooped into two vessels. No, our Tyrrhenean Sea here isn't like the Adriatic, it doesn't have its colour. The colour here doesn't have the same depth. How can I describe it to you. The Adriatic has it. And now, here was this man from here by the Tyrrhenean Sea, who turns up in my city with eyes the colour of my Adriatic. How is that possible? Suddenly the Tyrrhenean Sea in his eyes turned into the Adriatic. They lifted from their seabeds and in a single moment the Tyrrhenean filled with the waters of the Adriatic, and the Adriatic with the waters of the Tyrrhenean. An exchange of colour, water, wave, and light. The names hadn't changed; it wasn't like with the seas, but with his eyes. The Adriatic remained in Split, and when I came here there was no sea but the Tyrrhenean.

I went straight home. I couldn't bear to stay out on the Riva and watch those eyes disappear forever. I told Yulia and Nevena that I wasn't feeling well and ran home. I had nowhere to hide, except in my aunt's room by the sewing machine. Fortunately, she wasn't at home. She was probably somewhere out on the Riva, searching for news about my uncle, to find out whether what we had heard was true, that he had died in the battle of Sutjeska, along with many others from Split. A wounded Partisan who'd managed to come back alive from the battle of Neretva thought my uncle had died there, but he wasn't certain. I opened the sewing machine and took out two left-over scraps of a blue fabric that I think was from some old bed sheets, and, as if in a trance, I cut out two circles resembling eyes, measuring them with my fingers and my eye, and I bordered them with green thread. I held them in my hands and kissed them, first one, then the other. All of a sudden, I heard Krsto down below. 'I'll kill her!' he was shouting. 'Now I'm really going to kill her once and for all! I'm not going to bite her; I'm going to kill her!' He was shouting like a madman. I tossed the eyes into the drawer beneath the sewing machine shelf and went downstairs filled with rage. My father was standing there, my mother, too, and when they saw me, they literally grabbed Krsto so he couldn't attack me. 'You would wipe the blood of that fascist! He's the one who broke my finger, he's the one! Because of him, my finger's just dangling there, and it'll be like that for the rest of my life!' Krsto kept shouting, but I kept quiet. I really hadn't imagined that the soldier whose blood I wiped with my handkerchief would be the very one who had tormented my brother, the one who, while he was drunk, had grabbed something like a bottle opener and broken the little finger on my brother's left hand so badly that it really would hang limp his whole life. I didn't recall his name from when Krsto came back all bloodied. I think he told me, but I don't remember. Now he just called him a fascist. I ran upstairs to the upper floor, locked myself in, and waited for my aunt to come home. I spent the whole day sitting up there with her. She silently embroidered five-pointed stars onto caps. I took out the eyes I'd made, looked at them a moment, and then with trembling hands that caused the needle with red thread to poke my fingers, in a quiet that not even my aunt disturbed, I too embroidered caps for the friends of my uncle whom we hadn't seen for two whole years. We didn't even know whether he had died in the battle of Sutjeska, Neretva, or some other battle, that was his alone, a battle of life and death.

On 15 September 1943, just a week after Italy's capitulation, the new anti-fascist Italian brigade *Garibaldi* defended the city from the Germans who had penetrated Split. Grandma Nedjeljka could not stop thinking of the soldier with those large eyes. She was sure he was gone. He was no longer on the Riva. If he really was a fascist, as Krsto described him, then he would certainly have gone. He had been waiting for a ship. He wasn't among the other soldiers who were rustling about wondering, it seems, whether to go or stay. But then, even if he had considered staying, after that incident with his ear, he'd certainly have decided to go. What would he do in a place where someone hated him that much? Grandma felt she had lost something she didn't even have, but something she felt more and more that she could have. It was as if her soul had left her body, that's how she felt, she told me. It was as if her body moved by itself, lay itself down, as if her hands sewed and embroidered of their own volition, and her legs simply moved themselves, the same as that time before the war when she saw the skeleton in the high school biology lab—that is how she now felt, like bones that move muscles by themselves, not through her will or desire. Every day she looked at those eyes of blue fabric bordered with green thread, then returned them to the drawer beneath the sewing machine. She did not exchange a single word with her brother. Once, when she ran to Yulia's, she saw Yuri with a young woman, a girl, more precisely, in the lane by St. Duje's Cathedral. He acted like he hadn't noticed her. He must have been ashamed, not so much by this romantic encounter as by what happened with the soldier in the harbour. Grandma Nedjeljka often felt like going to Charlotte's to see little Marcel, and to speak with her French teacher, but she was always overcome with shyness, an awkward feeling that she shouldn't bother them. It seems that the respect she felt for her French teacher during those war years became for her a feeling about the importance of respecting the privacy of one's elders. But one day her father asked her, 'Neda, did you buy 'Free Dalmatia'? I heard that the first Split edition has been published.' 'Why didn't Krsto bring it? After all, he and Yuri were selling it!' she wondered. To satisfy her father's wish, she got up the courage and went to her teacher's. She knew that she'd find a copy of the paper there that Krsto had evidently not brought home for their father on purpose. They would surely have it. Of course, Charlotte embraced her and laughed saying, 'Non-Oui, Non-Oui, everything will be fine.' Marcel played with her hair and repeated 'Non-Oui, Non-Oui,' the only words he knew.

AH, NEDI. Until the end of the war, I kept that copy of 'Free Dalmatia,' the first Split edition number 28 that my teacher and Charlotte had given me, the edition that published The Call to Arms by Elio Francesco, the First Commander of the Garibaldi Brigade: 'Comrades, let us fight against those who subjugated your Fatherland and mine!' Papa reread that speech a hundred times. He felt terrible at that time, even though he wasn't suffering from any illness: it was as though a sense of foreboding was eating away at him, something tormenting him, but what? To the end of Papa's life, I never understood what worm was gnawing at his soul. We were all celebrating, rejoicing in Italy's capitulation, though that lasted only a few days. A week later the Germans began to attack. We still had no word about my uncle. Nearly all our neighbours who had stayed home now joined the Partisans, especially when they saw what the Italian soldiers —those who had remained in Split and decided to become anti-fascists—had done. Cross my heart, it was only later we learned how, at first, those new Partisan regiments weren't given weapons but often served as medics, technical support, drivers, or mule drivers. Only the former Carabinieri were allowed to fight and were able to form the Garibaldi battalion. But, instead of a cap with a five-pointed star, they wore red scarves around their necks. I don't know, at the time it seemed the most natural thing to me that if someone had already decided to fight for your side, they needed to have weapons, and not be subordinate to the others because of mistrust and doubt, yet, this business about giving them scarves rather than caps seemed funny to me. Still, when Italy surrendered, I wore a hat, not a scarf. 'You never know,' my mother would say, but Papa merely gazed at the newspaper articles. Exhausted, but without any obvious illness, he sat on the chair in the kitchen and, for the hundredth time, read the first edition of *Free Dalmatia* that was published in Split immediately after the capitulation of Italy. He had not sung 'Marjane, Marjane' for a long time. Outside you could hear the bombing that had been going on for two weeks already. We were afraid to stay in the house, afraid it would crash down on our heads and bury us in the basement, and so, along with everyone else, we ran to Diocletian's Palace and hid in the underground rooms. Before this, the only time I had been down there was with Krunoslav and now, now that I was hiding from the bombs, I felt like I had returned not to the scene of romance and my first kiss, but to the scene of a crime. If love could be called a crime. Krsto disappeared, twice, even from there, and, when he came back a few hours later, he was carrying dead fish. 'Where are you going and what are you getting into? This running around of yours is taking years off my life,' my mother said to him. 'I jumped into the sea with the other kids and pulled these fish out. They were bombed.' 'Did Yuri jump in, too?' I asked sarcastically, unable to look at the fish with their red eyes. 'Yeah, he did. So did his father.' 'Good Lord, what won't this war drive you to do,' my aunt muttered. Even when we were staying at home, Krsto would go out, then tell us yet again, that the city was full of dead Italian soldiers who had been targets of German bombing while waiting for the ships to take them back to Italy. 'What about our soldiers?' my aunt always asked. 'There were some of ours too, but I don't know which ones exactly because all of them have their heads cut off.' We suffered through our time in the underground room, all of us with our own thoughts. Then one day towards the end of September an idea popped into Papa's head. He went down to the basement with a bucket of rainwater he had scooped up by the drainage pipes. He washed, shaved, and put on one of the few articles of Partisan clothing still at our house from the last time Krsto returned home without handing them over to his connection with the Partisans; he put a cap on his head, kissed all of us on the forehead, and without a word went into town. It would have been better if he stayed home that day as well, just as he had all those years! My mother wrung her hands, I sighed but said nothing, my aunt could barely keep Krsto from running after him: 'We've already lost one man, and now two, so you want to go and be the third?' she told him, and I know Krsto felt flattered—he had always felt like the man of the house, even when he was a child. We learned later that Papa had set out in the direction of the shooting we could hear, towards Poljička Street. He had decided to join the Partisans at last. But, near the church, a bullet from a random Italian soldier found him. The soldier, starved and faint with fear, had been frightened by Papa's shadow on the wall of the church and fired. The bullet mowed him down right there, but not on Poljička street, where eight Partisans fought to the last with the Germans. After the war, Krsto said to my aunt one day 'Tito praised everyone, but not Papa.' I thought to myself—look what my brother has been living with all this time. Look what has been tormenting him! Tito praised the Partisans who had fought on Poljička Street, but not our father. They had become national heroes, but not Papa. For me, there was something more important than my brother's troubles and that was to tuck the first Split edition of 'Free Dalmatia,' into my hope chest as if it were some precious thing that my father had loved while he was still alive.

AH, NONNA NEDA, Grandma Non-Oui, it's a good thing you and Nonno Carlo aren't alive. Granddad is surely turning in his grave because the dead, who were then alive, know everything and are the first to learn about everything. Even the Italian media reported it. I came across several newspaper articles about it today in the bookstore. You probably know this already: in Split the day before yesterday, someone drew a swastika and wrote *Gott Mit Uns* on the memorial plaque to the *Garibaldi*, granddad's *Garibaldi*. What a turn of history! Unfortunately, there aren't any copies of 'Free Dalmatia' in the bookstore. Who would read it here in Sicily? That's why I always read it on the internet; I've gotten in the habit of reading Boris Dežulović's column at least once a week. Although I don't know him, I feel his articles are the most truthful and relate, somehow, to our life. Another journalist wrote about the swastika, under the headline: 'Vandals, do you know that the Garibaldi defended Split against the Nazis?' I couldn't resist reading the comments below the article. One, in particular, stuck in my mind. Someone with the tag *gentlmanst* wrote something like: In Split it is hard to find a single street, entry to a building, or even an elevator on which someone hasn't drawn a swastika. He proposes that the branch of city government in charge of tourism should intro-duce Nazi-tourism, because there is no other city where Nazism has grown faster than in Split. He proposes some guy named Luka, whose last name I don't remember, as a guide. Is it really true that Split is a centre of Croatian Nazism? It's interesting that where there are good soccer teams there are a lot of Nazi-fans. Nationalism is already one step toward Nazism. It should be the other way around, shouldn't it? But then, why is there the saying, 'A healthy spirit in a healthy body?' The body is healthy, but the spirit is, apparently, sick.

AH, NEDI, several evenings after June 3, the day of the worst German bombing—someone counted as many as 12 bombers that flew four times over the city, the city literally crumbled with ruins and the dead—Krsto came racing home. He was shouting as he came through the door, his voice hoarse: 'They've taken the teacher away!' 'What teacher? Where?' my mother asked, but I knew immediately that he was talking about the French teacher, my teacher, or, more exactly, Charlotte's husband, Marcel's father. 'They took him along with some other people, mostly women and children, but some other men, too; the Ustashi kicked them and shoved them into a truck.' 'What about Charlotte?' I immediately asked. 'She wasn't there,' he said. Charlotte wasn't there when her husband was taken away by the Ustashi? That seemed strange and unbelievable. Surely, she would have come out and sworn at them to prevent them from taking him away?' And in her arms, two-and-a-half-year-old Marcel, who could scream and cry in Croatian and French. But why would the Ustashi take pity on him? Would they even care what she said? These unconnected thoughts swam in my head; something stronger than pain gripped my heart. I couldn't take it; I put on one of Papa's old coats and set off running towards my teacher's neighbourhood. I didn't think for a moment what I'd say to Charlotte when I saw her, or why I had come. I'd just ask her where they took my teacher. Did I, a former student, have the right to know? But—that meeting on the Riva when Italy capitulated and Charlotte embraced me with Marcel in her arms, and, several weeks later, when my teacher came to my father's burial in Sustipan, because he was the one who had found my father's body while walking past the lane by the church and had dragged him home to us, into our courtyard, unable to say a single word. These gave me the strength to go and ask what had happened. From the basement windows I could hear Marcel crying. I didn't even knock; I just went inside, opening the bar on the door sharply and quickly. I think they were frightened for a second, I heard Charlotte's cry, but when she saw me, she was confused at first, then said to me, 'Neda, they took Vid away. They discovered he was Jewish on his mother's side. They took him away.'

I had never known that my French teacher's background was Jewish. He never once said anything about it, and we didn't know anything about it. Once I met his mother and father at a mass in the nearby church, 'St. Mary of Health.' How, then, could his mother be Jewish? Maybe I should have guessed, but I was too young then to connect his interest in Jewish culture and Jean Jacques Bernard's play *Martine* which he loved so much that we performed it, in French, no less, every Christmas and at the end of every school year. Generations before us had also performed it, and some of us, instead of calling him 'our French teacher' called him *Martine*. He knew the play by heart. He would recite it standing behind the last bench in the classroom, first asking us not to turn towards him, but to just listen to his voice. Perhaps there was a *Martine* hidden in each of us? I even played the title role once. If someone had asked him why he liked this play so much, he would have said, 'It's not just this play. I like other plays as well, but I feel like I wrote this one myself.' But now, had one of my classmates betrayed him to their fathers, or some other Ustashi? During the earlier years of the war no one had touched our teacher, but now they had come after him, a yellow star in their hands, which they threw at him as if he were a dog, and then dragged him from the basement room. Charlotte had been with Marcel in the inner courtyard of the house, framed by the walls of the surrounding houses, the only piece of land and sky where they felt a bit protected from the outside world. My teacher had no chance to shout out. The door was closed, and the inside of the room was not visible from the outside. His parents had gone to church; his mother had long ago converted to Catholicism. At home, they never talked about his mother's Jewish background, but Vid's library held many Jewish writers. Now he had been discovered. The Ustashi gagged his mouth with the dust cloth that hung on the chair, and one of them pasted the star to his forehead with spit, but as they dragged him out, the star fell, and as Charlotte came into the room with Marcel and didn't see her husband, she ran to the door and there on the threshold she caught sight of the gold star. Everything was clear. Charlotte told me all this in just moments, hugging Marcel in her arms the whole time and sobbing. I told her that I hadn't known he was Jewish, because I didn't know what else to say. 'He never talked about it,' she said, 'and in some way, he wasn't. His mother had become Catholic at a young age, and Vid was baptized in the Catholic faith. But that's irrelevant when Ustashi boots march into the house. When I saw how many Jewish authors he had in his library and asked him about them, he said, 'This is my national literature.' 'He loved *Martine*,' I added, and she nodded and stroked my face. 'Neda, do you think they'll let him go?' That is what she asked me. Charlotte, a journalist with *Figaro* who had moved to Split for love, a woman a million times more learned and more intelligent than I was. My first thought was, 'No.' I knew about other Jews from Split who had still not returned home. Still, I said, 'Yes.' 'Non-Oui, Non-Oui,' whispered Charolotte, but her eyes were so full of tears. Not even the sea beyond the Riva held as much water.

NONNA, Nonno Carlo said only once that he had been a fascist before he became a Partisan. Maybe he was a little tipsy, I don't know, maybe he was so upset he couldn't control himself any longer. You surely remember better than I do the day we learned that terrible piece of news, the worst in our extended family. It was the day before my sixth birthday, a day I had been antic- ipating for months, on account of the present Papà promised me—my first-ever bicycle. I was playing with Margherita here in the courtyard while you and Granddad were drinking coffee. I recall that Granddad Carlo said to you; 'It's so nice to drink coffee outside.' I learned later that there had been a police raid in the town that day and a number of Mafiosi had been caught. That meant that for at least a few days there would be peace with no gunshots. It must have been several weeks before Margherita nearly drowned which had a happy ending for her, but an un- happy one for Granddad. Suddenly, out of nowhere, Uncle Mario came crashing into the garden. He hadn't called or written that he was coming, and no one was expecting him. 'Mario, where did you suddenly pop up from?' Granddad shouted so loudly that Margherita and I turned towards the garden gate. 'Son, what's the matter?' you said. Margherita and I were delighted; children never expect anything bad when someone comes visiting out of the blue. I ran to him and gave him a hug, and he gave me one too, and then, smiling, he lifted Margherita in his arms. He was carrying a small blue bag, but no gift of any sort. This was already cause for alarm. In our house, no one arrived empty- handed, without at least something for us children. Especially our uncles who lived so far away—'on the continent', as our

Granddad would say—so we would know ahead of time when they were coming and we would spend weeks getting ready, and so would they. They arrived with wondrous presents from Trieste or Rome, especially Uncle Luca who had money, but no one to spend it on. But now here was Uncle Mario from Trieste with nothing but a small bag which clearly held no hidden presents for me and Margherita. 'What's happened, son? Why have you come without letting us know?' you asked again, as you gave him a kiss. 'How can I tell you,' he said, sitting down at the table, as we gathered around him. Mamma and Papà were still at work. 'I don't know what to say, it's hard to tell you,' he said. 'It's Antonio...' 'What's the matter with Tony, Nonna's handsome one? He's big, a man and a half already!' you said, but for me, my cousin Tony was neither big nor handsome. Whenever he came to visit, always without his half-brother Marco, who spent his school breaks with his Grandma and Granddad on his mother's side, Antonio would annoy me, asking a hundred times an hour, 'Si o no, no o si? Per que no, per que si?' And sometimes he'd add, 'Only stupid people have a name like yours and Nonna's.' He wanted to pinch Margherita and me and to break the branches of the orange tree, just like that, for no reason, just to destroy something. When he was at our house, I could barely wait for him to leave, but for Uncle Mario, the best uncle in the world, to stay. And now, here was Uncle Mario sitting in our garden, which used to be his as well, and all he said was: 'Antonio, how can I tell you this, I think he's, he's a Nazi...a neo-Nazi.'

AH, NEDI, how can I forget. Right away you asked: 'What's a Nazi?' and Margherita repeated the word over and over several times: na-zi, na-zi ... 'What do you mean, a Nazi?' your Granddad asked. I could sense the huge lump in his throat. 'Just what I said, a Nazi,' Mario repeated. Mama's poor boy. It was so difficult for him to tell us, us, his parents who had endured all the dangers of Nazism and Fascism, in reality, during the war. Your

Granddad even more so; after all, his parents were Fascists in some way, brain-washed by Mussolini's ideology, and they had raised him in that spirit and sent him to the army. 'When?' I asked, as if I were looking for a reason that would cause Antonio, a 17-year-old, to become a Nazi. 'I don't know. We got a call from his school to come to a meeting with his mother. The director sat with us in the office and said: 'I don't know whether you know this or not, but Antonio is a neo-Nazi. He doesn't even hide it here. He's formed a Nazi association of students at the school and he makes a special point of using threats and violence to recruit students younger than him.' That's what Mario said, unconsciously imitating the director's voice, which was a bit higher than his own. He and your aunt just sat there as if they'd been knocked over and they didn't say a single word. The classroom teacher added that for the past two years Antonio had become increasingly strange, especially in the way he dressed, and she hinted that they had allowed him to dress in 'Nazi-style.' Apparently, it had never occurred to them that Antonio hadn't shaved his head because, as he told them, he'd gotten lice at school, but because that's how his friends looked. They all wore black, military-style boots even on the hottest days, and wore a swastika on the sleeve of their jackets. 'That's how young people dress nowadays, there are more and more skinheads, but your Antonio made flyers calling for the organization of a high school movement "against everything that isn't Italian,"' is what the director said, or that's what Mario said he said. Granddad stared at your uncle as if staring at a scarecrow, he couldn't believe what Mario was saying. 'But why?' was all he asked. 'Why?' repeated Mario. 'Who knows why? Maybe because he has everything and doesn't know what to do with himself. Or maybe because Marco is better than he is in school and has a completely different character. He's involved, shy, an excellent student. A few days ago, Alessandra told Marco to wake Antonio up for school and when Marco went in to wake him, Antonio kicked him in the stomach.

I wanted to strangle him, but Alessandra defended him: 'Don't,' she said. 'Mario, don't, it's my fault, I shouldn't have sent Marco to wake him, I forgot that he told me he wasn't going to his first class.' 'But that's not all,' Mario added, 'He's especially cruel to me. He tells me I'm not pure Italian, he tells me that my blood is dirty, with Slavic cells and that such mixtures make him want to vomit.' Mario then told him: 'Since I'm mixed, that means you are too, we'll never be pure Italians, just so you know.' But Antonio answered him: 'I am a pure Italian. I don't acknowledge your mother, the schiava-slava. And,' he added, 'because of her, I don't acknowledge you either; I'll kill someone if I have to prove that I'm pure Italian. I want to be pure like my great grandfather was, your father's father.' Ah, Nedi, I thought I was going to vomit, I felt so sick from what I was hearing, and Carlo turned as white as a sheet. Mario could no longer carry this on his own, I guess, and he told us everything that had been weighing on his soul. Your granddad's hands began to shake, he was so upset; I placed my hand in his, pressed it tenderly, and said to Mario: 'Mario, my son, it's not important what Antonio thinks about us, what's important is to turn him from the path he's on. That's all that's important.' 'But how, Mamma?' he said, 'He already attacked a kid, one of the Slovenian minority in Trieste, right in front of the Slovenian primary school. He attacked him and took his boots, literally took them off. The boy had to walk around barefoot until he went home. The story was written up in the local newspaper, but they didn't name the person who had done it. We found the boots, a child's size, at home under Antonio's bed.' Ah, Nedi, your Granddad and I couldn't believe what Mario was saying. You and Margherita sat there listening, Margherita simply repeating a word from time to time. We didn't even think about going into the house to bring out something to eat or drink. It was only when your parents got back from work and were also surprised by Mario's visit, that we treated him like a guest.

THEN, while Uncle Mario told Mamma and Papà some brief details, he literally begged them to let him send Antonio to us over the holiday, to get him away from his bad group of friends and these ideas. You and Granddad Carlo nodded yes immediately, but I began shouting: 'You can't, you can't, I don't want him, I don't want him...' I was screaming loudly, and I think it was the first time in my life I fought against something so cruel, so treacherous and, because I was just a child, my spite grew; I literally threw myself on the living room floor that evening while we were sitting there listening over and over to my uncle's stories. There was no way I wanted Antonio to come that summer and live here with us, for us to be afraid every day of his violence and abuse, and have him keep shouting crazily at me: 'What are you, si o no? No o si?' And I especially didn't want him to come and kill you, Nonna. You, more than anyone else, stood in his way of being 'pure Italian' even though I didn't know what being pure Italian meant. I kept shouting and crying, and no one could calm me. Mamma said several times, 'Out of spite,' until finally Uncle Mario said, 'I'll call Luca, maybe it would be better to send Antonio to him in Rome; I've heard there are NGOs there that help rebellious young people like him. Besides, Luca understands these things, parents of children like him go seek his advice. Maybe Antonio will get over his Nazi-ism there.'

Good, I said to myself. The next day when I got up Uncle Mario was no longer there; he had caught the plane from Trapani to Rome, heading to Uncle Luca's to ask his help. You, Granddad, Mamma and Papà were still worried; Margherita was busy playing, and slowly the house regained the peace that had completely disappeared with Uncle Mario's visit and his news, the worst in the world for our family. 'What an odd fate you have!' you said to Granddad: 'You, a Partisan, and your grandson a Nazi. Why must we endure something like this, Carlo?' But Granddad Carlo only mumbled: 'A Partisan, yes. But before that I was a fascist. Maybe it's in his genes. Maybe Antonio will change, too—who knows.'

IT WAS ONLY RARELY that I could drag a word out of Granddad
Carlo about the anti-fascist war in Yugoslavia, even though
I really wanted to hear his side of the story about the events
connected with Grandma. But I was too young to make him tell
me, and even if he had, I don't know how much I would have
remembered. He didn't speak for the last two years of his life,
and I was eight years old when he died. I would still feel now
that he had carried a secret to his grave if I hadn't found the one
and only remaining letter he wrote to his father who had lived
in this house until he died. His mother died while he was at the
headquarters in Bačvice. He sent this letter from Zagreb on 10
May 1945. Here is what he wrote in quite a formal tone:

'Dear Papà, no matter how much you don't agree, congratu-
lations are due to us for our victory over Fascism! Although the
fascist ideology appealed to you and Mamma, which is why you
sent me to Mussolini's army, I want to tell you that my entire
being no longer contains a single drop of fascist ideas. They have
evaporated like rain drops and I have come to understand that
these ideas were never mine, but yours and those of our neighbours in Castellammare. As you know, here in Yugoslavia I have
fought on the side of the Partisans as a member of the Garibaldi
battalion. I already explained to you in my first letter after
Mussolini's capitulation why I became a Partisan. Then, later,
even Sicily was liberated from Fascism to your greater or lesser
regret. I hope that Mamma has come to understand at least in
the next world that Fascism is evil, nothing more. What's more,
I hope during these past two years your anger is gone and that
you will be waiting for me in good health. I've already told you

that our battalion joined the first Proletarian brigade. We fought everywhere, from Split to Belgrade. That's like crossing all of Sicily on foot. At some point during the summer of '44 we found ourselves in Sandžak, and a well-known Partisan commander, Plavi appeared and told us Italians that we could either go back to Italy by way of Split, which had already been liberated, or we could march towards Belgrade. There was a personal reason that was driving me towards Split: when Italy capitulated, I saw a girl there wearing a red beret. She has stayed in my memory, and she has been my guardian angel in every battle against the enemy. But love takes a back seat in wartime, and I was sure I wouldn't find her. You wouldn't be happy if I brought home a wife from here and Mamma, if she were alive, would have liked it even less. You're probably still hoping that when I get back, I'll ask Enio's daughter, Angela, to be my wife. Even though we all know her father is in the Mafia. I didn't tell her to wait for me; I hope that by the time I get home she'll already be married to one of her father's co-workers. That girl in Split is the only one still on my mind. I found it hard that it was the eighth Dalmatian Corps that liberated Split and not us. Had I been there on the 26 October, I'm sure I would have seen her again and I would have recognized her immediately by that red beret of hers. I'm sure she was wearing it again! Still, she's got no reason to fall in love with me. Quite the opposite, she probably just hates me. The reason for that—I'll tell you when I get home. I feel terrible writing about such things.

Still, when they asked us whether we wanted to go to Split and head home or continue on to Belgrade—even though I thought I might see her again on the Riva—I shouted out loud with all the others: To Belgrade! The Germans were far better armed than we were, but when you want something, anything is possible, isn't that what you told me when I was a child? The hundreds of kilometres we traveled on foot were nothing compared to the freedom of the capital city of Yugoslavia. On

October 22, 1944, together with all the other troops, we liberated Belgrade. There were more than 15 thousand Italian prisoners of war there. When they heard us speaking Italian some of them cried like babies. Joined with soldiers from all the other brigades, we freed them, too. The people of Belgrade took us into their homes to take care of us and feed us. Even Tito appeared in the Belgrade parade. You'll hear more about him. He singled us out, the Italian Partisans, for special honours; right in the middle of Belgrade, he stopped the Italian brigade, our Garibaldi Battalion, along with Partisans from the Mateoti Battalion, and gave us a special greeting. Then we set off again to the west and we continued fighting for months in areas that were still not liberated, until we finally reached Karlovec which was liberated on May 7th, 1945. As for Zagreb, where I am writing to you now, we liberated it yesterday. You must know by now that Germany surrendered yesterday. Don't take this hard because brighter days filled with hope are now coming for Sicily. We just need to root out the Mafia, but the Allies are going to help with that as well. From now on things will be different. I think I'll be heading to Split soon and from there, God willing, I'll sail home to you. Death to Fascism!'

AH, NEDI, I had never seen that letter from your Granddad. You children always did know where to look; God himself couldn't keep anything hidden from you, so how could a person like your Granddad Carlo. It's interesting that he didn't write to his father the reason he thought I'd hate him. Clearly it was because of Krsto. After all, wasn't Carlo the soldier who broke the little finger on Krsto's left hand so badly it would never fully heal? That was when Krsto and Yuri were going to sing Dalmatian and Russian songs to the soldiers.

But fate takes its own course. Or as Charlotte would say to me: 'Non-Oui, irony is always bigger than life.' She was, of course, thinking of her own life, about the fact that she, a Parisian, a journalist with *Figaro,* left everything to come to Split, but her luck lasted a short time: it wasn't just that the war started, but the Ustashi took away her husband, my beloved French teacher, just a few months before the liberation of Split and he would never return home. Charlotte still didn't know which concentration camp he died in. Some said Jasenovac, others that the Ustashi had handed him over to the Germans who sent him to Treblinka.

In my life, Nedi, irony was larger than life because of my brother, Krsto. When I met your Granddad, whom I had, in fact, chosen, even though logic said I shouldn't be with someone who had treated my own brother so horribly. But does the heart know logic? Those beautiful May days of '45 after the victory over the Germans and the final liberation of Europe, we were all caught up in the excitement. The Partisans who had survived returned home, but not my uncle. My aunt waited for him every day, from morning till night. She started to go a bit crazy; she talked to herself and no longer wanted to do anything. I felt an irresistible desire to sew, at last, the dresses from that first faded fashion magazine Charlotte had given me and from the others she gave me later; after they took her husband, Charlotte had no will to live, let alone a desire for dresses and fashion. But I was young and felt it was time for me to be a young woman, a mature woman; I was 22 and didn't have a boyfriend, or a husband, or children, just like most of my girlfriends—after all, there were almost no men in the city, they had all gone off with the Partisans. Now they were returning from far-off places and fronts all across Yugoslavia—though many never returned. Including my uncle. One day my aunt simply gathered up her clothes, a few small objects, and photographs, put them in my uncle's old wooden suitcase, said goodbye to us, and left our house saying, 'I'm not a widow and I'm not divorced. It'll be better for me to go to my mother's in Samobor, she's alone, old and sick, at least I'll be able to care for her.' After she left, my mother and Krsto never mentioned her, it was as if she hadn't lived in our house, but I missed our sewing together quietly in the room on that upper floor where no children's voices were ever heard. Now, the upper floor was left empty, so little by little I moved my things up there, I got rid of the bedding and replaced it with new sheets, and I began to sleep in my aunt and uncle's bedroom. Krsto and my mother stayed below; I would go down to help my mother prepare dinner, and after we had eaten together, I would take myself to 'my floor' where I would sew and sew, ever more interesting dresses and skirts for me and my friends, and, after a while, for their relatives as well, in exchange for meat and milk, and later for money. Life returned to the city together with new fabrics in the stores that were open once again, and the poverty that had eaten us to the bone during the war was hidden beneath the shelves of fish and other types of seafood in the fish stores and among the olives and mandarins at the market. My mother started taking vegetables to the market again. I missed Papa and his fish that could be smelled throughout the whole house. His boots, which long ago my aunt had tripped over, causing her to miscarry, still stood beside the hooks and fishing nets in the nook behind the door. Krsto often went fishing but he always wore his own rubber boots, though he wore the same size as my father. This bothered me, so one day I collected up the boots, hooks, and nets and brought them upstairs to my floor, and left them in a corner in the hallway. We didn't talk about Papa very often: who knows why we felt this unpleasantness, embarrassment even, when we thought of him. It was as if we couldn't make sense of his life or his death. Why didn't Papa have a clear point of view in his life, or in his death? He didn't join the Partisans, he didn't go out on the square when Italy surrendered, he hung around the house all those years, hiding with us in the basement or waiting for a bomb to strike him at the kitchen table, and in the end, when he decided to go and fight, a stray bullet by a random Italian soldier killed him. Even today, it's still not clear to me whose side he was on: ours or no ones?

ON MAY 15, 1945, the Split harbour was teeming with Italian soldiers from the Garibaldi and Mateoti brigades who were preparing to sail to Italy. People were handing them flowers and something to eat, round loaves of bread, bottles of olive oil, a jar of fig preserves. Grandma Nedjeljka was out with her girlfriends all wearing the new dresses she had sewn—the first dresses like that on the Riva. Looking at it today, I'd say they were on the prowl for husbands, but at that time, even though they were driven by that same hunting instinct, they were just beautiful Split girls who had come to greet their defenders in the war. Some soldiers sat cross-legged at the harbour, others stood and hopped in place, everyone excited by the departure, the trip ahead that would take them back to their native towns.

Granddad was there, leaning on a mast which had two flags fluttering: Yugoslav and Croatian; he stood and looked around, probably looking for the girl in the red beret. But why would Grandma be wearing a red beret in May? She had let her hair down, its dark chestnut colour the same as mine, sparkling in the sunshine. But there were many other girls like Grandma, and even today people say that the girls from Split are all beautiful the same way, as if they had stepped from a women's magazine or fashion catalogue. Granddad Carlo looked and looked but didn't recognize Grandma Nedjeljka anywhere. She recognized him, of course, by those large eyes that were like no one else's. She once said to me: 'The only one with eyes like your granddad's is Mario.' Blue, large eyes filled with the Adriatic—not the Tyrrhenean—Sea. In a flash, Grandma separated from her friends and ran towards him. And when Carlo saw her, all he said was, 'Is that you?' and she said, 'Yes, it's me.' In Croatian. Then she added in Croatian: 'Aren't you the one that broke my brother's finger when he was singing for you at the headquarters in Bačvice?' 'Yes,' Carlo whispered, having learned Croatian during those years, not very well, but enough to be understood. And so, mixing Croatian and Italian, he added. 'That was me. I'm so sorry. I was drunk... I was in pain... I had just gotten a telegram telling me that my mother had died on her way back from church...innocent, caught in a Mafia crossfire on our street in Castellammare del Golfo...' That's what Granddad Carlo said. And Grandma asked: 'Are you going home to Italy?' 'Yes, to Sicily, my father's still there.' 'Can your father take care of himself?' 'He can, why?' said Carlo confused by the question. 'Then, you can stay here,' Grandma said to him. She would always laugh when she told me about it: 'I didn't know then who was talking for me, God or the devil, but it certainly wasn't me.' She gestured, signaling him to stay, so he would completely understand. The next moment, Granddad Carlo set off with her, or more precisely, after her, after that beautiful figure in the

93

new, flowered dress; it was only when they got to her house, weaving their way through the crowd, that they told each other their names.

AH, NEDI, throughout my whole life I haven't been able to fathom what was happening to me at that time. I still ask myself who spoke those words in my name: God, the devil, or me, myself? When people fall in love, they do unbelievable things. It was the same with me: I brought Carlo to our house. As soon as we went in, Krsto recognized him, by those eyes that no one else had, and he began to scream, shouting: 'Are you normal? You're bringing home the guy who broke my finger, the fascist?' 'Partisan,' I said loudly and clearly. But Krsto got right in his face, ready to hit him: 'Now that you're here at my place you'll see what I'll do to you.' He grabbed his right hand and wanted to twist his little finger, but Carlo, although skinny, was strong and muscular, battle had steeled his strength, and in one stroke he twisted my brother's arm and while Krsto kept screaming from the pain, I led Carlo upstairs to my floor, calling back loudly, 'From now on Carlo will be staying here,' and I locked the door behind us. But when Carlo and I were left alone I was gripped by girlish shyness, something you've probably experienced, if, that is, your generation still knows what it means to be shy in front of a young man. Carlo was confused and upset by his meeting with my brother, and so was I. Really, that's all the two of us were thinking of, not about one another or about love, and those things. It's only in movies that things happen like you expect them to: as soon as the door closes behind them, the two young people strip off their clothes and hop in bed. But not us. He stood in the living room and didn't know whether or not to sit down, whether he should go, or whether he should say something, but I closed the windows, went into the room where the sewing machine was, put a new sheet on the bed I no longer slept in, because I had taken over my aunt and uncle's room, and I called loudly from that room: 'You can sleep here.' He didn't answer, he just stared vacantly while I searched through everything looking for a clean pair of my uncle's pyjamas and any other clothes of his still up there. All Carlo had was his Partisan uniform and the military boots he had taken from a dead German soldier. I remembered my father's fishing boots. 'If they fit, you can wear them,' I told him. 'When you go fishing.'

GRANDDAD CARLO lived in their house, that is, on Grandma's upper floor, for just a few months. During that time, he would often go fishing wearing her father's boots, and he'd come back with so many fish that she or her mother could whip up some new dish, and what was left, she'd take to the fish market and add them to her Uncle Simo's stand to sell along with his. They didn't eat together: Grandma brought half the food upstairs to her floor, and half she left for her mother and brother. Other than swearing, her brother did not utter a single normal word to her, and every time he encountered Carlo, he'd curse his mother in Croatian. 'He doesn't have a mother, you idiot!' Grandma Nedjeljka would always answer, but he'd just call her a bitch. Granddad tried to avoid encountering Krsto and their mother. She didn't know how to relate to him, with warmth as a son-in-law or coldness as someone who shamed the family. Her daughter had brought him home, but he hadn't said anything about a wedding, or marriage. A woman who followed her own will was unheard of in Split. People gossiped about Grandma —not just her acquaintances and their neighbours on the street, but also the men who were back from their time as Partisans. Even though Carlo had also been a Partisan, they always referred to him as 'The Frog-eater,' as Italians in Yugoslavia were then called. 'That Frog-eater has moved in with the Jagnić family. He's going to knock up Neda and leave them something to remember him by. It's a good thing her father isn't alive.' People said all kinds of things, but Grandma hadn't even kissed Carlo. One day Yuri came into the kitchen, turning up unexpectedly after a long absence: his family had taken refuge from the Germans in the refugee camp on the Island of Vis. Yuri had begun singing and acting in an art and culture club but when the family learned they would be sent to Egypt, to the El Shatt refugee camp, they slipped away at night by rowboat and returned to Split. Yuri also recognized Carlo as soon as he saw him—after all, before Italy's capitulation he and Krsto had gone together to sing Dalmatian and Russian songs. But Yuri's reaction to Carlo was different from Krsto's: he burst out laughing. He laughed loudly, hilariously, so much so that Carlo relaxed a bit and smiled. Then Yuri began singing a Russian song that he had sung in the headquarters back when Carlo was still a fascist. Krsto's forehead furrowed in anger, but he didn't want to interrupt Yuri. Maybe he was afraid he'd lose him, Yuri, his only friend. When Yuri finished the song, Carlo held out his hand to him. After that Carlo and Yuri became friends, despite the difference in age between them. Yuri began to come to the house more frequently, sometimes even with his accordion, and he sang Russian songs, and Carlo sang Sicilian ones, until the day Krsto said to Yuri: 'That's enough! Don't ever let me catch you here again!' and he took the accordion and threw it out the door. Yuri left, upset and bitter, sadness in his eyes. So Krsto was left without his only friend. Grandma Nedjeljka said that this is what he was like his whole life. A misanthrope can't stand other people. A misanthrope can only be alone. A misanthrope can't laugh at life or cry at death.

AH, NEDI, how happy those days were when Yuri came to our place. Songs, accordion, music, Carlo finally felt human. But everything sweet is short-lived, isn't that right? As always, our Krsto spoiled everything. How can misanthropes cope with normal people? And how do we cope with them? Carlo and I were still living upstairs on my floor, I sewed in his room while he was out fishing alone out below Marjan. We ate upstairs and afterwards, I would usually continue sewing, because I now had customers who would come to try things on, and Carlo would have to stay shut in my room, daydreaming, and waiting for

97

them to leave. There was a woman who needed her dress in a hurry: she said she was going to her sister's place in Dubrovnik; they hadn't seen each other for four years, ever since the beginning of the war. I worked only while Carlo was out or when I explained to him that I had to work, so long as it wasn't bothering him. It never bothered him. Then one morning, I couldn't wait any longer for him to leave the room, I went in, and opened the sewing machine. Carlo was either still sleeping, or just waking, I don't really know. I had never seen him in the morning before he got up. I was in love with him, but numbly, as if I were cast in plaster or bronze. My heart would pound constantly whenever I was in his presence, but now it was pounding somewhere deep inside, outside of its normal place. My legs were tired, my hands exhausted, my head heavy. It was a strange love, wasn't it? I was never certain what he felt. But that morning, while I slipped the thread through the sewing machine needle, I took a good look at him. He was covered with a light summer blanket that my aunt had made, blue, cotton, not like my satin one. One of his feet was visible, big, rough, marked with wrinkles. I stared at that part of his body and some unknown force lifted me from the chair, drew me to the bed, and stretched my hand towards his foot. I tickled it. Yes, I tickled it, just like my father had tickled my foot when I was little when he would wake me for school. Carlo moved his foot, not under the blanket, but outside it. His muscular ankle was now also visible. I tickled him again. Then he shook, threw off the blanket, leapt up, and when he saw me, he reached out and pulled me towards the bed, hugging me with his whole body and covering me with kisses. Along my whole body, and the soles of my feet. What happened next you know yourself, you're not a child. You too must have felt in heaven when a man's penis pushed inside you. It was the first time in my life. I, nearly an old maid, and he, a man who had served with the Partisans who surely had some sexual experience, but I don't think a lot. He never told me, not even later, how many girls he had had before me, or whether, perhaps, he had made love with some of the female Partisans. But I understood how young we both were, innocent in every respect, but already aged by life.

NONNA NON-OUI, how romantic that was. Even though you would always say to me, 'What do you mean romantic! It was dangerous, not romantic! My mother and Krsto on the floor below, us on the floor above them. The door to the upstairs left unlocked. Krsto never went upstairs, but Mama would just drop in whenever she wanted, bringing us tea or figs. Yes, and a customer could show up, that woman, for example, the one I was sewing for so early that morning, before Carlo had gotten up.' Surely your romantic encounter took place at the right time in the right place. Even though you never told anyone about it. No, no that's not true, the only one you told about your love was Charlotte, the day she unexpectedly showed up at your house with Marcel, now already three-years old, clutching her hand. Charlotte was still young, but sad, so sad; there was no one sadder. She had remained in Split after the war, although Vid never returned from the concentration camp. His parents were old and barely managed to care for Marcel while she wrote articles for the French paper *Le Monde*. She no longer worked for *Figaro* after it changed its political stance. When she appeared at the door and your mother opened it, Charlotte tried to smile as broadly as she could. Your mother simply shouted upstairs, 'Neda, Charlotte!' And you, in your confusion, dropped everything and came running downstairs and when you saw Charlotte and Marcel you began to hug them as if they were the closest people to you in your whole life. In fact, you didn't have many people close to you, but Charlotte was near and dear to you, even though you had actually seen her only few times in your life. She said that she had brought you some new catalogues, the newest fashions from Paris; her sister had sent them. You told her that she should come up to where you and Carlo lived rather than staying downstairs. Carlo was out fishing at that time and, while Marcel played with spools of thread and bits of cloth in the room with the sewing machine, you and Charlotte sat together in the living room and the first thing you asked was whether she had heard anything about her husband, your French teacher. 'Nothing,' she said. 'We still don't know whether he died in the gas chamber or from hunger.' Who knows which is the better death in a concentration camp. 'Will you and Marcel stay in Split?' you asked her. 'Yes,' she said, 'as long as Vid's parents are alive. I can't leave them. Marcel is their only joy; they no longer see or hear very well, and my father-in-law can't get out of bed any longer.' And she told you that she was writing short articles for *Le Monde*, sending reports and information about Yugoslavia after the war. The French were particularly interested in Yugoslav Communism. 'And what are you doing, Non-Oui?' she asked. And like a shot you told her about Granddad Carlo, how you were in love with him, that he was from Sicily, that he had at first been a fascist at the Bergamo headquarters in Bačvice, but then had become a Partisan in the Garibaldi Brigade, and you even told her about the incident with Krsto and how you had been the one to invite Carlo to live with you, and that you were lovers and lived like husband and wife. You even told that to Charlotte, without shame; she was Parisian, after all. Even though she had lived many years in Split, she still had progressive ideas about life. 'Vid wouldn't judge you if he knew,' she said as she hugged you and said that you had to live your life here and now; nothing else was important. 'Will you go to Sicily?' she asked, and you didn't know; Granddad Carlo hadn't said anything about that, things were better for him in Split: he had a home, he caught fish, dinner was waiting for him at home, and at night—a bed with a woman who loved him. If it weren't for Krsto's provocations, one could say that, after the war, Granddad Carlo was living like a pig in clover.

AH NEDI, that October 26th turned out to be a cursed day rather than a holiday. It was warm that day, not like the year before when Split was liberated and there had been torrential rains like never before. The whole city was once again out on the Riva to celebrate the Day of the City, the first-year anniversary of the victory over Fascism, and it was the first time that Carlo and I had gone out in public as girlfriend and boyfriend. My mother was there with some of the neighbor women, and Krsto was most likely out by himself. After his quarrel with Yuri, he literally did not have a single friend. He hadn't made any new friends either in his first year of high school. I sometimes saw him wandering around on his own. Carlo and I got all dressed up and headed out to the Riva. I don't know why, but once again I put on Charlotte's beret. It wasn't cold, quite the opposite, it was a warm October day, but now I marked celebrations in Split with the red cap I wore the day Italy surrendered. I kept it in a special box covered with dried rose petals, so it wasn't hard for me to find. Carlo, with those big eyes of his, told me I was the most beautiful girl in Split. But about marriage and children, he said nothing, and with my feminine pride, I couldn't ask him, though it was on the tip of my tongue sometimes. On the square there was singing, speeches, and chanting of 'Death to Fascism, freedom to the people.' Everyone was in a holiday euphoria. When one of the speakers said that Split would also remember those residents who had not returned from the concentration camps throughout Europe, I caught sight of Marcel in the air above people's heads. Charlotte had lifted him as a sign of approval. A few minutes later she drew near us and said that she had seen my red beret in the crowd and then she met Carlo for the first time. Several times she held my wrist and whispered to me kindly: 'Non-Oui, Non-Oui.'

It had been a year since the city of Split had been liberated and normal life was slowly returning. When the main celebratory events were over, Mama came up to us and said that we'd be going to the cemetery to pay our respects to Papa. 'I just need to find Krsto,' she said. As Carlo and I were saying goodbye to Charlotte and Marcel and to my girlfriends, some now with boyfriends, and Nevena with her fiancé, my mother and Krsto arrived. For the first time ever Krsto was wearing a cap with the word 'Hajduk' on it; he had written it in pencil. My mother said, 'I could barely drag him away, he was off drinking with those *Hajduk* soccer fans; they're all older than he is.' We pulled ourselves from the crowd and set off to the Sustipan cemetery. Krsto turned to Carlo several times, saying: 'You motherfucker! Why are you coming to my father's grave?' And he again cursed Carlo's mother. 'My mother is dead, Krsto,' Carlo said to him quietly and calmly. He didn't want to challenge Krsto or even talk with him, but whenever Carlo was agitated his Croatian got so garbled that even I couldn't understand what he wanted to say. 'You should be dead, too, you should've been dead a long time ago,' Krsto screamed at him. I grabbed Carlo by the wrist, while my mother merely sighed because of the altitude, because of Krsto's words, because of all of us. Carlo said nothing and kept walking. This irritated Krsto even more and he said: 'You broke my finger, but I'll break your neck.' 'God forgive him,' my mother whispered, but my anger and hate towards my brother was seething. I did not know how much one could hate one's own brother. It's impossible to hate someone not related to you so intensely. No. It's only someone close to us, someone we should love, that we can hate to such a degree. When we drew near the grave, Carlo held back a bit to give us some time to be with our father. My mother cleaned the grave and sobbed, while I silently told Papa that I was here and that I had brought Carlo along so he could meet him, and it was as if I could hear my father's voice ringing in my head: 'A fascist and an anti-fascist.' Yes, that was a correct formulation. Carlo had at first been a fascist, then became an anti-fascist, but what did Papa want to tell me? I stayed silent just as I would have had he been alive and had said the words aloud. Here I was, his alive daughter, feeling confused beside my deceased father. Krsto circled the grave strangely, nervously. 'Take off your cap,' my mother said to him quietly. 'Has Neda taken hers off?' he shouted back. 'When she takes off her stupid red beret, I'll take mine off.' 'Men take their hats off at graves,' Mama whispered to him, gritting her teeth. 'But children don't,' muttered Carlo. What possessed him to say that, my quiet Carlo, who was always so careful around Krsto. Everything grew dark in front of Krsto's eyes. The next instant he was swinging at Carlo's head with a wooden cross. The wooden cross from our father's grave! We had driven that cross—two planks of wood nailed together—into the ground when we buried Papa, a wooden cross with ribbons the colour of the Croatian flag and on the cross the years of Papa's birth and death. From top to bottom it read: Stipe Jagnjić, and from left to right: 1896-1944. With the cross in his hand, Krsto kept swinging at Carlo's head and body, running after him around the grave and through the other grave sites, his fifteen years filled with anger and unusual strength. My mother grew pale and collapsed on the grave, crying out: 'Krsto, Krsto, may your name be devoured, you don't respect the cross or your father!' I was also in shock, and I ran after them and grabbed Krsto's arm, but he was remarkably strong, and he was beating Carlo like he was out of his mind. Suddenly the top part of the cross broke and fell off. Together with the letters S and T of Papa's name. Only then did Krsto stop hitting Carlo. Carlo was covered in blood. He dragged himself to a bush, where he dropped down, supporting himself with his last ounce of strength. I thought that he was going to die, that he would breathe his last after the beating he had just endured.

Krsto, the cross still in his hand, bent down and picked up the broken piece. He tossed both pieces and ran from the cemetery. I don't even know how we got back home that evening, how my mother and I held Carlo up. We pounded the cross back into the ground, and attached the broken piece with the small piece of rope we found tossed on the ground near the grave, but the board sagged, covering the letter T. The ribbons were torn. Back upstairs, in our room, Carlo let flow a torrent of tears, without saying a word. All through the night I put compresses on his bruises and his wounds. The next day he gathered the few things he had into an empty flour sack and said to me: My soul will stay here with you in Split, but my body has to go back to Sicily.

POOR GRANDMA NEDJELJKA, nothing worse could have happened to her. Granddad Carlo went home to Sicily, to a small
town with a long name—Castellammare del Golfo, but Grandma
remained in Split, no one's girlfriend, no one's wife, nothing.
She wasn't pregnant, although her mother kept looking at her
belly. But her belly did not grow and later there was no reason
it would. Confused and unhappy, Grandma spent days staring
into space or shedding tears larger than the drops from the
Adriatic Sea during a blustery storm. She never left the house,
until her friends began dropping by to see her, but even then,
they couldn't get her out on the Corzo, to a dance or any other
get-together—and they pitied her, they comforted her, but
Grandma Nedjeljka felt better when they weren't there. There
is a sense of schadenfreude people have, especially those who
are close to us in some way, not so much among blood relations as among friends—though in Grandma's case she had no
worse enemy than her brother—yet, sometimes in her friends'
company she sensed their strange, hidden pleasure from her
own unhappiness. As for her mother, she didn't say anything
at all, for her it was as if Carlo had never existed, hadn't until
recently lived in their home, and as if Krsto hadn't attacked
him, nearly killing him with the cross from their father's grave.
'God forgives,' was all Grandma's mother repeated for days and
months. Charlotte would pass by with Marcel every once in a
while and she'd deeply empathize with what had happened to
my Grandma. She never forgot to bring one of the new fashion
catalogues her sister had been sending her for years from Paris.
Ten years older, Charlotte was to Grandma both a friend and

a mother. And Marcel was dearer to her than Krsto had ever been, from the day he was born. 'For us French, there is a nuclear family: parents, brothers, sister. But here you're all family, cousins, aunts. How about your family, Non-Oui?' Well in Grandma Nedjeljka's family it wasn't like that. Not even her own brother felt like part of the family, and there were no ties with other relatives. Her uncle never returned from the war, her aunt had gone to her mother's in Sombor and never sent a single card or letter, even though she and Grandma had been close during the war years. They had no other relatives in Split. 'You are my relative, of the first degree,' Grandma Nedjeljka said to her, hugging her as she left. And Charlotte repeated: 'Non-Oui, Non-Oui' and cried for Grandma Nedjeljka, for herself without a husband, and for Marcel without a father. It was easier for Grandma to cry about Carlo in front of Charlotte. But there was no solution for either of them. Carlo sent a telegram from Sicily: 'Body arrived home. Stop. Soul no. Stop.' But not another word more: no 'Come, we will get married' or 'How are you' or 'Why did things turn out like this.' During the nights Grandma reached for his body and said to herself, 'At least if I had gotten pregnant, I'd have had a living gift from him my whole life.'

NONNA NEDJELJKA, Grandma Non-Oui, it seems that's not what fate had written for you. Isn't that what people say where you're from? Before New Year's just one other telegram arrived from Granddad Carlo: 'Krsto should have broken my neck. Stop. It would have been easier for everyone. Stop.' What were you to make of a message like that? It wasn't a letter, just a statement. You wrote him a letter. You wrote about what you were doing, how you were sewing, and that you didn't talk to Krsto at all, that you saw Charlotte from time to time, and that your friends came to visit; your pride kept you from adding: 'And what about us?' If I been in your place, I'd certainly have written that to him. In the 21st century feminine pride is considered an old-fashioned virtue. I read somewhere that more and more young women are proposing to men, or they make the first move. To tell you the truth, I've seduced two or three of the men I've made love to, I even just up and asked one of them if he wanted to do it with no strings attached. The world in which we live has changed. But then, after the war, the world changed in a different way; there was no time for romantic exchanges. You kept waiting for a letter from him, but Granddad Carlo simply didn't write letters. When he wanted to tell you something, he sent telegrams. Five or six words—that was it. And then you would keep thinking about them for months.

Announcements about the activities of WAF, the Women's Anti-Fascist Front began to appear in Split. All the women and girls who had still not joined the movement were invited to help in building a new society. Some of Grandma's friends joined and went to the regular meetings of the Split branch of the WAF. Grandma went with them once. Then she kept going. Since she was already known in the city as a seamstress, she was given the task of teaching young women the craft. Girls came to her who wanted to learn to sew so they could get jobs in the NIRS factory and soon Grandma's floor was turned into a meeting place filled with women's voices and the sound of their footsteps. This turned Grandma from her dark thoughts. In the meantime, several of her friends had married; she sewed their wedding dresses and felt a bit envious of them. After the liberation of Split one of them had moved to Italy with a former Italian soldier who, like Granddad Carlo, had become a Partisan. One day in 1946 she turned up at Grandma Nedjeljka's. 'Mira!' Grandma couldn't believe it. 'Aren't you in Italy? Did you come for a visit?' 'No, I've come back. I ran away,' Mira told her. She hadn't come to talk about herself but to order some slacks and a skirt because she had arrived with almost nothing from Italy. 'But why?' Grandma asked, as something was squeezing her soul. 'Just because. Because it wasn't what I expected. Angelo brought me to his home in a village, Vogogna, a beautiful village, but with strange people. First, they couldn't get used to a foreigner settling there and they kept calling me Yugoslavia, as if the whole country had moved to their village. But that was nothing, that wasn't the problem. The problem was Angelo's family. Living all together in one house were his parents, his brother with his wife and children, two younger sisters, his grandmother and grandfather, plus his old bachelor uncle—twenty people in a house with three rooms. When I arrived, they gave me gold jewelry, which was their custom, and for the wedding, they said, I'd also get pearls. We planned the wedding for the next month. Angelo spent all his time with the men, in their tractor repair shop, and we women were either in the house or in the olive fields. I wouldn't see him all day. His sisters, his mother, his brother's wife—they all lectured me: all in Italian—though I've known Italian since before the war, they didn't talk in their village like in the book—they lectured me about housekeeping, how I had to dress, how I had to wake up at night and cover him if he was uncovered, how the mother was the most important person in the life of her sons, not me. Angelo was a dishrag and wasn't allowed to speak up. Once at lunch everyone kept teasing me because I had put salt instead of sugar in the coffee, and even though I told them it was a mistake, and it wasn't my fault that the sugar bowl and salt cellar were identical, they didn't stop making fun of me while Angelo said nothing, just kept his head down. I wanted to get up and leave right then, but something told me not to rush. A few days ago, two full weeks after this happened, I told Angelo I wanted to go to Split to get a few things before the wedding, to say goodbye to my parents and have a party with my girlfriends. I told him that no one entered a happy marriage without this party with her girlfriends. Angelo didn't suspect anything and three days ago he sent me off by bus to Milan, and from there I continued to Trieste, then caught a boat here. Just one suitcase, nothing unusual. But inside it I packed everything of value I owned: along with their gold as payment for everything they had done to me, my nick-nacks, and my dresses. I didn't have room for my slacks and skirts, and I couldn't take everything with me; it would have made them suspicious while they waved goodbye from the yard. And now I'm here and I'm not going back. I sent Angelo a telegram today with three words: 'Not coming back.' And to tell you the truth, my soul feels lighter, even if people here call me a divorcee. So, you take care, don't go flying off to that Carlo, so the same thing doesn't happen to you as happened to me.' That's what Mira told my Grandma while she was measuring her waist and the length of her legs. And she thought to herself: Mira sends telegrams, too, like my boyfriend. Angelo must certainly have been shocked by those three words. His family was probably relieved, like Mira. And everyone probably said to him: 'I knew it, I wouldn't trust a foreign girl as far as I could throw her.'

AH, NEDI, Carlo wrote to me again towards the end of '46. In the telegram, he wrote: 'Father died. Stop. Mafia here. Stop.' How could anyone respond to such a telegram? I responded with a telegram. 'I'm sorry. Stop. Your Neda. Stop.' And then, nothing. For months, nothing. I went to all the WAF meetings, and all the leaders were pleased with me. I taught many young women to sew. But some of the older women began to ask me why I didn't get a job at NIRS; I shouldn't be working at home sewing for money; it wasn't in the spirit of the Communism we were building. I had no answer to that. 'Comrade, we will need to sanction you,' one of the leaders said. 'You are enriching yourself on the backs of the poor girls in the city. Either sew for them for free, in the spirit of Communism, or don't sew at home anymore.' I had been giving a huge discount to everyone, I was sewing, earning just enough for us to get by, and for my love of sewing, but then I began to sew for free. I really did want

109

to contribute something to the country we were building. I told everyone who arrived with fabric that they didn't need to pay me, because I couldn't accept it, I didn't want to sew for money. But the people I knew well would leave me some money or some other form of payment always surreptitiously, without saying a word. Silently, because I knew people were spying; my mother told me one day that she had found my slippers scattered on the front steps, but I never left them like that. 'That means someone was upstairs while you weren't home. But how did I not see them?' my mother wondered. We practically lived on my sewing and on the vegetables and fruit from the trees in the garden that my mother took to sell at the market. I hadn't continued going to school, I felt too old for high school, and I felt some reluctance about going to the night school for adults. Krsto didn't want to go fishing anymore and didn't contribute anything to the family finances any other way. 'He's young,' my mother said, though she had not said that when he truly had been young. So, I was lucky when one of my customers would secretly and silently leave me some eggs or a bottle of milk or something else for the sewing. But I felt that I could achieve more than just sewing. I decided to educate myself and I began to read books on all kinds of subjects. I began visiting Charlotte more often and to borrow books from the library of my French teacher, for whom we were still grieving. How many Jewish authors he had in his library! No, he did not have books about Judaism, or a Torah, there was nothing connected with the Jewish faith, but there was poetry, prose, and plays, in French, German, and English, as well as a few in Croatian. Aside from the Croatian one, I could only read the ones in French. The books that made the greatest impression on me were the *Tropismes* by Nathalie Sarraute, which Charlotte had ordered from Paris in 1940, and of course my teacher's beloved play *Martine* by Jean Jacques Bernard. Not even Charlotte had known that some of the authors were of Jewish descent, but when she looked at the books one by one, and read most of them, she understood that her husband truly thought that Jewish literature was his 'national literature' as he had once told her. Who had unmasked him, who had betrayed him to the Ustashi who took him away forever? We never found out, but there were people living in Split who had all sorts of beliefs and convictions: there were Ustashi, and Fascists, and Partisans, though there were also some who had remained neutral.

I read other books, too, about history, geography, biology, everything that came to hand, I felt the need to complete the education the war had interrupted. At the WAF meetings I always begged the more educated women to bring me a book. They most often brought me books about socialism, women's rights, and about the new measures society must take: most of these were pamphlets rather than books. I took them, I kept them at home and returned them at the next meeting. They told me to sign up for night school, but I excused myself because of the girls who came to me for sewing classes in the evening. Some looked askance at me, but others brought me real books or textbooks. I gobbled them up, reading everything, forgetting about my womanly sadness, of the love that, like a branch in the breeze, waved before my eyes like a dream, not reality. Carlo got in touch so rarely and only by telegram, that I also stopped writing letters to him. I thought time would eventually heal the wound. I began to go out with my girlfriends, after the WAF meetings we would often go to dances, get-togethers, evening dances. Freedom knocked us all in the head: we would rub our eyebrows with shoe polish to make them darker, and our mouths with crepe-paper to redden them. When I went out, my mother would snap at me: 'So now this. You've already lost your honour with that guy. A shame to the world.' Still, she wasn't as strict as my friends' parents—when a woman's honour was in question they made no exceptions, so they didn't allow their daughters to wear eye-catching dresses, just long skirts. Because of that, the young women would hide in their handbags their dresses that, most often, I had sewn for them and we would go to Bačvice and change into our dresses behind the trees and rocks and hide our other clothes under the stones on the beach. We laughed out loud as we walked on the Riva, did silly dances on the bandstands throughout Split, and cried out loud at the movie 'Song of the Adriatic' at the Tesla movie theatre, and on December 26, 1946, we got dressed up as if for a celebration and crowded in to the 'Karaman' theatre to see the new big movie screen. But there were only a few of us friends still unmarried; the rest were already taking care of children at home, working in the factories, and, in their own way, contributing to the building of socialism. I had my admirers, some a bit older, and even two younger men, all of them back from the war and all of them knew, of course, about Carlo and the fact that he had lived with us a few months, and also about the incident with my brother Krsto: in a town like Split it took just an hour or two for everyone to know everything. I rejected them all in turn, I never danced with young men, most often I would sit watching my girlfriends dance with their chosen ones and gripped by a sadness that seemed endless, distant, a sadness that physically hurt and spiritually broke me in pieces. I hated Krsto from the depths of my soul; he was truly the one guilty for all my unhappiness. After '45 when Hajduk became the top team in the republic, he never took his cap off his head—a new one now, with *Hajduk* embroidered on it—and it always reminded me of the scene with Carlo at the cemetery on Sustipan. It was his fault that Carlo was gone and that I was left without love or happiness. But on December 31, 1946, I received a telegram from Carlo: 1947—wedding. Stop. Sicily. Stop.' I looked at the telegram and I didn't understand the message, I kept thinking how he had written *Sicily* and not *Castellammare del Golfo*, which is three words, but Sicily only one, so he didn't have to pay as much for the telegram. A wedding? Whose?

AFTER GRANDDAD SENT THAT STRANGE TELEGRAM, which the clerk at the wicket in the post office in Castellammare read aloud and wondered what he was trying to say, he knew that Grandma Nedjeljka would have a hard time understanding it, and even if she could understand that it was about their wedding, not someone else's, that didn't mean she would accept. A wedding without a proposal? So, he sent another telegram, the longest one of his life which caused the woman who worked there to regard him with a mixture of amusement and pity: 'Would you like to marry me? Stop. Wedding in April next year. Stop. You will move here. Stop. I love you Non-Oui. Stop.' Aha, now everything was very clear to Grandma Non-Oui. She looked at the telegram, turned it around in her hands, and in her brain echoed those two small words of her nickname: Non, Oui, Non, Oui, Non, Oui, Oui. Rather than running downstairs to tell her mother, she slipped her shoes on as fast as she could and raced off to Charlotte's with the telegram. Charlotte was there, holding a letter with a seal and signature. Before Grandma could tell Charlotte her news, Charlotte showed her the letter which contained written confirmation: Her husband had died in the concentration camp in Jasenovac. There it was in black and white, signed and sealed.

AH, NEDI, how insignificant my news seemed in comparison with hers: she received confirmation both that her husband was dead and where he had died; black on white. Now there was not a crumb of hope that he would appear at their door someday to their great anticipation and surprise. I think that it was because of that possibility or that illusion, whichever it was, that Charlotte hadn't left Split with Marcel after the war. And there I was, holding a telegram offering marriage. Life had ceased to offer joy to Charlotte and Marcel, while it now offered happiness to me. I hid the telegram under the belt of my dress, turned my eyes from the letter, and took Marcel in my arms; he was already big and heavy, and, in a quiet voice, I sang him a little French song, the one I sang to you, too, when you were little: 'Frère Jacques, Frère Jacques, dormez-vous?' Marcel continued the song since he knew it by heart. Charlotte looked at us, dazed, sighing deeply. She silently dragged herself to her room. I sat a little longer with Marcel, smiling at his grandma who was seated in the old armchair, motionless, lost, but still alive. His grandfather had died a few months earlier, never knowing precisely where his only son had died. Unbeckoned, the thought came to me: what meaning is there for Marcel's grandmother to be alive? She can no longer see or hear, she doesn't recognize Marcel, she is now nothing but a difficult obligation for Charlotte. Her son died too young, but she is still breathing the air, she would see in another New Year's, but wanted none of it. Isn't it better for some souls to find their death in this world when the body is already nearly in its grave? But the soul doesn't give up so easily and is not released so simply. I left Charlotte's without telling her about Carlo. As I returned home that melancholy day in Split, that last day of 1946, I had already made up my mind. Yes, Carlo and I would get married in Sicily. Yes, Carlo loved me. Yes, I loved him, too. It was, in fact, that simple. It was as if all that remained of my name was the 'yes' part, DA, while the 'no' part, NE, was carried off on the last day of 1946. Or was it?

YES, NONNA NON-OUI, it is simple when you know who you love and why. It's even simple for Margherita who knows that she loves Pietro. But it's not simple for him, he has a wife and children. If you ask me what I love, and more importantly, whom I love, I wouldn't even know how to answer you. Neither would most of my friends. Friendship, going out, having sex with some tourist or other, promises that we'll see one another again, even though that's all meaningless. But you knew: There was Carlo, and that was it. Although you had been separated a whole year and still would be for several months, it was decided: Carlo—full stop. For him, it was the same: Nedjeljka, even though he hadn't seen you for a whole year. You didn't even know what his life was like in Castellammare del Golfo, what he had been doing the whole year, those telegrams of his didn't tell you anything about his everyday life. Yes, his father had died, but that was the only information you received about his post-Split life. And, that the Mafia was there, but everyone knew that—how could the Mafia not be in Sicily when it had been there even before the war? Did he live alone in the family house, had he had other girlfriends? What, in fact, did he do for a living? Had he been going out with that Angela from the Mafioso family? And more importantly-what were you two going to live on after you moved in with him? His father had had a cobbler shop, and, even though Carlo finished school, the most natural thing for him to do would be to work there. Yet, now with his father gone, had he closed the shop? You had a pile of unanswered questions, yet nothing was more important for you than the fact that in April you would get married in Sicily. You didn't even consider how you would get there, or whether your mother would come to the wedding (as for Krsto, it was clear to you he wouldn't), or what you would do once you got there, how you would earn a living, not to mention the fact that you didn't speak Italian. That's what frightened you the most. But a woman can get herself organized and be practical a thousand times more than a man if she's motivated, at least that's what contemporary guidebooks for a happy and successful life say. And that's what you told yourself: I'll sew my own wedding dress; I can sew for customers there as well, and maybe Carlo already has a sewing machine in the house, if not, we'll buy one, I'll take the money I've saved with me. I'll start studying Italian today. You pushed all the other books aside and began to study Italian from old newspapers, dictionaries, and books. You picked up a word here, a grammatical rule there. That New Year's Eve, much to the surprise of your girlfriends, and your mother, you didn't go to the celebration on the Riva but there, tucked under the blanket that had covered Carlo, you studied the words: *amore, amore mio, grazie, arrivederci, non capisco*.

ON JANUARY 1, 1947 Grandma told her mother she was going to marry Carlo in April. 'April what?' her mother asked. She didn't know herself. She waited for the holidays to end and then sent Granddad Carlo a telegram. 'April what? Stop.' '20 April. Stop.' Granddad Carlo answered. 'On April 20th,' she told her mother. 'The girl's getting married just so she doesn't have to sit around the house' her mother whispered, because she, along with all the neighborhood women already considered Grandma Nedjeljka an old maid with her honour lost. 'Well, maybe they're more progressive than they are here, and at least you won't bring shame on us any longer,' she added. Krsto had gone off to school, and she hadn't told him anything, but she was sure her mother had told him, because that afternoon she heard him in the house downstairs in the kitchen, pounding the wall with all his might. Something broke, most likely the old clock had fallen from the wall. Their father had saved this clock that had been his grandfather's, and even during the war he had carried it down to the basement, into their hiding place, to protect it from the Italians, Germans, and Croatian Ustashi. But just some bit of news like his sister's marriage to Granddad Carlo could drive Krsto out of his mind. But this time Grandma Nedjeljka didn't go down. She cleaned the suitcase she got from her mother, the one her mother had brought when she came from Rijeka to live in Papa's house. It was old, but beautiful, from the '20s. 'Rijeka fashion,' is what her mother would say. For three and a half months the suitcase stood in the bedroom, and Grandma Nedjeljka put in and took out different objects, photographs, dresses, skirts, and slacks. She'd change her mind, then return the objects again, especially the tied-up bundle of Krunoslav's poetry, which, in the end, she tucked in the scissor box inside the sewing machine case. But there was one thing that had been in the suitcase from the first day to the last: Charlotte's red beret. The box in which she had put new dried rose petals every year was too big for the suitcase, so she wrapped the beret in the only piece of silk left from her customers. The beret would sit atop all the other items, even as she changed things daily. For three and a half months. Finally, there, beside the beret, lay her wedding gown, sewn in the latest Paris fashion, according to a pattern from the most recent fashion catalogue that Charlotte had given her. 'Non-Oui, this is Dior's New Look, presented just two weeks ago in Paris. My sister sent it by express mail. No one else will have a wedding dress like yours.' And Grandma Nedjeljka sewed her bridal dress, an ivory satin that Charlotte had presented to her personally, for the wedding, she said. How and when she got it from Paris, she didn't say. In fact, even the brides of Paris could only dream of such a bridal dress with a skirt, ten metres wide, calf-length, with a tight waist and fitted bodice. The dress weighed a ton and took up almost the entire suitcase. But Grandma Nedjeljka said to herself: 'I won't even need my other dresses there. I can just sew them again.' Placed under all the other items in the suitcase was the one edition of 'Free Dalmatia' she had saved from the day Italy capitulated, in September 1943, the Split edition that her father had read a hundred times, which carried *The Call to Action* by Elio Francesco, the First Commander of the Garibaldi. 'Comrades, let's fight against those who subjugated your homeland and mine!'

NONNA NEDJELJKA, Grandma Non-Oui, who would have thought that you'd move to Sicily! First a boat to Trieste, then a bus to Milan, from Milan to Genoa by bus, and from Genoa to Palermo by boat. You were seen off at the harbour by your mother, your girlfriends, and only two of the older women from

WAF who hadn't believed your brother when he turned up at one of the last meetings you attended and began shouting: 'Kick her out of WAF! She's in love with a former fascist who broke my finger in '42! He didn't like our Dalmatian music and he beat me up because of it! Fascist! She slept with a fascist in our house and now she's setting off to marry him!' and he showed his dangling finger to the women standing around him, while flipping you the raised middle finger of his other hand. Nearly all the women activists were shocked. They believed him and after a hasty hearing they took measures to punish you: you had to sew 50 workers' coats for the new employees in the cement works. Before you left for Sicily that's all you did, and when you had finished the last blue coat, you told yourself you were clearly not born for the WAF, and that perhaps it was due to those genes from your father who seemed absent during the most important events marked by Croatia and Yugoslavia. Even though you had sewn Partisan uniforms with your aunt during the war, the WAF leaders not only made you sew those coats after their snap judgment of you, they also publicly declared you a 'traitor to the people.' The two WAF women who had come to see you off had somehow managed to drive Krsto from the hall but now were not at all pleased with your decision to leave Yugoslavia, although, you did promise that you would send them as many articles and books about women's rights in Italy as you could. Charlotte also came with Marcel to see you off. Krsto did not, especially after that WAF incident. You didn't even care whether they excluded you from their ranks or not; your leaving for Sicily was also welcome from that point of view. As the boat set off, you caught sight of Krsto hidden behind a palm tree that had recently been planted on the Riva. He didn't wave or look in your direction, he just stood there, a tall, secretive, young man of 17 years. And, for the first time since everything had happened between you, you felt sorry for him—really, more for yourself and your relationship with him. But there was no chance of conversation or forgiveness. Sometimes it is simply too late in life, regardless of those who say it's never too late. You traveled in a daze; you didn't look around, take in the seascape around you, or the cities you were traveling through for the first time in your life. This was something quite different from my generation; for us, if we have the money, we like traveling more than anything else. On April 19 you reached Palermo. Granddad Carlo was waiting for you and as you came down from the boat, he seemed older to you, as if you hadn't seen him for ten years, though, in fact, it had only been a year and a half since you parted. Maybe you also seemed more mature to him, a bit older, but whenever I asked: 'Nonno, how did Nonna look to you when you saw her for the first time in Sicily?' he would just say 'Beautiful.' Surely that meeting must have been both confusing and passionate, but in your words, the way you told it, you just hugged, kissed, and then, riding on a motorcycle with a trailer that his father had left him, Granddad Carlo brought you to Castellammare del Golfo.

AH, NEDI, on April 19, 1947, I arrived in Castellammare; Carlo drove the motorcycle while I rode behind holding tight to his waist, the suitcase inside the trailer. I felt like the trip to Carlo's small town lasted for hours. As we got closer, the first thing I saw was the sea, the Tyrrhenean Sea, its colour so different from the Adriatic, but a sea, a sea nonetheless, and I remembered what Charlotte had said to me: 'You're going from sea to sea. That's the best way. I went from land to sea, which was lovely, but to go from sea to land is the worst.' She was right, yes, I had moved from one sea to another. But I must tell you, throughout my life I've missed the blue of the Adriatic, which simply can't be compared with the blue of the Tyrrhenean. Even though I often went swimming with my girlfriends at Bačvice after the war, the sea was less about the water for swimming than a place of colours, sounds, waves, quiet, and love. The

Tyrrhenean also had its sounds, its love, but it was different than the Adriatic. The panorama of the little town came into view: the fort by the sea, churches scattered along the narrow streets, houses sparkling in the April sun. Carlo and I arrived here, to this house, which hasn't changed much from what it was then, despite the few renovations we made over the years. The garden is the same, though instead of the orange tree, there was an olive tree growing here. We planted the orange tree that autumn the olive tree collapsed, maybe from old age or moisture. Most of all, I loved this yard, this garden. Inside, the rooms seemed large and bright when I opened the windows, but Carlo immediately ran over to tell me that in their town windows were never opened, and often, not even the shutters. 'No one here opens their windows,' he said to me. At first I was surprised, but I quickly understood.

Everything in the house was old, just as his parents had left it. I went to open my suitcase in the living room to take out the wedding dress right away; it was all I had thought about those days I was traveling, worrying that it would get wrinkled and be ruined before I could wear it. Then I remembered that Carlo wasn't supposed to see it, because that brings bad luck to a marriage, so I asked him to carry the suitcase into one of the other rooms. The wedding dress remained in good condition, as did the beret. I brought Carlo a very simple present from Split: the epic *Judita* by Marko Marulić. I was a bit surprised myself that I had chosen this gift, since Carlo never gave me any indication that he read books. I guess I took it more for myself than for him. To have something of my own, something Croatian, while I was living in a foreign country. I realised quite quickly that Carlo had pretty much forgotten Croatian and that's when it dawned on me why he hadn't written me letters, only telegrams: it was easier for him to tell me what he was thinking. I already knew basic things in Italian, so that's how we spoke, mixing the languages, since he had remembered some Croatian words. Then, he abruptly said: 'The wedding is tomorrow, at "St. Mary's" just down the street. But Neda, when I wrote to you, I didn't know that tomorrow there would be the first regional elections in Sicily. You arrived and Sicily became autonomous!' and he smiled as he embraced me. 'You know, people will be voting even here in our town. I'll have to go vote. The Socialists have got to win. This is a chance for Sicily and for Castellammare del Golfo. The Mafia is running our country. Things just have to get better after tomorrow.' And I thought to myself: 'It has to be better for us, too, after tomorrow.' That evening I slept in one of the rooms in the house, not with Carlo. After a year and a half separation, we felt a bit ashamed to sleep together. Before our marriage, before our church wedding.

WHEN GRANDMA WOKE, Granddad Carlo wasn't there. On the kitchen table he had left her two pieces of bread, a glass of milk, and a jar of orange marmalade. And, a note written on a sheet of paper, in telegraphic style, but without the Stop. 'At elections. Home at 12:00. Wedding at 1:00.' It was not clear to Grandma how they would get to the wedding, and who would be there, she wondered if there would be a godfather, and where they would have a wedding celebration, and whether he had invited any relatives or friends. She ate her breakfast, washed up, rinsing herself with warm water heated on a burner in the kitchen; she put on her wedding dress, combed her hair, put a white flower in her hair, looked at herself several times in the mirror in the bedroom which must have belonged to his parents. She picked up photographs of them one after the other; she saw only one photograph of Carlo when he was young, she looked at the various objects in the room, the clothes in the cupboards, the bedding wrapped in cellophane, and it was clear to her that this is how Carlo's mother had left the room many years ago before she died in that tragic way, returning from church and getting caught in Mafia crossfire. They killed one of their own, but struck her down as well, though she was absolutely innocent. Carlo's father hadn't moved anything in the house, he hadn't thrown away his wife's belongings, everything remained just as it had been and that's how he lived, waiting for Carlo to return from Yugoslavia, but soon after, he died, too. Was it also because of the Mafia? Yes, that's what Carlo had written her at the time: 'My father died. Stop. Mafia here. Stop.' But that hadn't meant that he died at the hands of the Mafia. He might have died a natural death of old age or illness. She decided to ask him, but not this day, their wedding day. The wedding dress was heavy and voluminous, but here was no one to help her get dressed. At twelve Carlo appeared dressed in a white suit with a blue shirt. At first all he said was, 'We'll see who wins the elections.' Only then he added: 'What a dress! Did you sew that yourself?' Grandma Nedjeljka nodded, a bit embarrassed that she had dressed like this, in that heavy Dior dress of ivory satin, here, in this small town. 'Come on, let's go,' Carlo said, and they set off down the narrow street towards St. Mary's. It was a good thing that Grandma didn't have a long dress that dragged along the street. The Dior New Look, the latest calf-length fashion, was just right for the cobblestone streets of Castellammare del Golfo.

AH, NEDI, there was no one outside the church. Carlo knocked at the door three times. You could hear the key opening the door, and there, inside, stood a man and a woman: 'Our god-parents,' Carlo whispered to me. They greeted me warmly and pushed a small box with the rings into Carlos's hand and all four of us walked to the altar. 'Lock the door,' the priest called out. Our godfather turned, went back, and slipped a huge brass key into the lock. 'Inside a locked church,' I thought to myself, and then, as if he had heard me, Carlo whispered: 'It's safer this way—with the Mafia, you never know.' The ceremony lasted a short time. The priest did everything himself, he sang, prayed, and did the blessings. At one point, he turned to me and Carlo and asked sharply: 'What question would you personally ask God if he were to contact you?' Then he stared at us waiting for an answer. I barely understood the question, but I had no answer. Or, I had only one: 'God, why have you never appeared to me?' which I somehow figured out to put into words but then barely managed to speak. Carlo said: 'I think something like that, too.' But the priest just stared back at our faces and said: 'No, those are not correct answers, the correct answer is a different question: "What can I do, Lord, to save myself?"' We were silent, but our witnesses began to cough. Finally, the priest said, 'For young people like you it is enough that you respect the ten Commandments and, above all, keep yourselves clear of the Mafia,' and then added, almost as if it were an order, 'Now, you may kiss.' Carlo and I kissed quickly, confused by the way the priest was acting. The priest escorted us to the door, wished us a happy marriage and many children, then turned the key behind us. 'Come on, let's go get some lunch at our house,' said Marco and Anastasia, and we raced almost at a run along the narrow street and came out at the seashore, where we immediately turned up another steep street. To enter their house, we had to pass through the atrium of another larger house. We went inside and Marco locked the door. 'There's no life here without a locked door,' said Anastasia who had evidently noticed how this locking of doors confused me. 'You never know who's behind your back,' Marco said, then added, 'But it's fine, we had luck today, with the elections, the Mafiosi are busy, and the town is calm.' I thought to myself, 'How am I going to live here? How will Carlo and I live here?' 'Now you are Lombardo, Nedjeljka. Nedelka, Nidelka Lombardo,' Anastasia said to me. 'I'm sorry, but when Carlo told us about you, I could never remember your name, it's going to be hard for you here with a name like that.' 'Nedjeljka in Italian is Domenica, but, just call me Neda,' I said to her, 'It's easier.' 'Or, Non-Oui,' said Carlo, squeezing me for the first time in a tight embrace.' 'That means Neda in her language. Ne and Da, No-Si in Italian. But in Split some of us called her Non-Oui, the name her friend from France gave her.' 'No, my French teacher,' I corrected him.

YES, NONNA NON-OUI, in the church of St. Mary's you answered Oui, Si. Without relatives, friends, without your girlfriends, without Charlotte, without your mother who did not want to accompany you and attend your wedding because she thought you were already too old to be a bride, and, without Krsto. Behind locked doors. You locked your doors all the time at home, too. At night, you also locked the door to the bedroom where you spent your wedding night, the room where I now sleep. A room that has witnessed several lives. But that first wedding night you felt like a virgin unveiling herself to her husband. You did not consider your lovemaking in Split a sin. I like that. And so, here you began your new, joint life. Even behind locked doors one can begin a new life. Freedom is, at least sometimes, solely spiritual. But here in this town you understood that freedom was something much more: it is life. In those elections Sicily elected its first parliament; the island had finally obtained regional autonomy. There were several representatives from this town as well, some somehow connected to the Mafia, but others were true fighters against it. One morning, before going down to the cobbler shop on the lower floor of the house, Granddad Carlo said to you: 'Neda, honest people live here behind closed doors. Behind curtains and shutters. In this town, there are too many Mafiosi to be able to walk wherever we want, go out for entertainment, or even to a store or church. We go out to the sea only two or three times a year. There are frequent fights in the streets, you'll hear gunfire and shouting. That's why this house will be your home, your city, your country. I'm down below with my shoes, but I need to tell you that I often have to make a pair or two for the local bosses. It would be better if you never came downstairs. Stay here on this floor, and at three o'clock every day I'll come up so we can have lunch together. I've oiled the sewing machine that my mother left, though she never learned how to sew. In the cupboard you'll still find silk and other material, needles, thread, everything you need for sewing. Make things for yourself, and later we'll find customers for you. But never forget what I told you: life goes on here behind locked doors...' That was the longest speech

Granddad Carlo ever made in his life. That's why you never forgot it. And you took what he said literally; you locked every door, not once, but twice. The shutters were drawn, but when you needed light for sewing, you opened them, pulling closed the blue curtain and then, from time to time, you peeked out behind it into the street. And, as proof that you had moved to a land where no one guaranteed anyone's safety, ten days after your wedding the biggest massacre in the history of Sicily took place; On May 1, 1947 in the village of Piana degli Albanesi, the Mafia ordered the rebel Salvatore Guilliano to take his band and attack the people attending Labour Day protests. Fourteen people were killed, including several children. Hearing the news on the radio you frantically repeated the announcer's words, words which otherwise you would not have learned or seen any need to learn them.

Instead of a honeymoon, every day after Granddad went down to his cobbler shop, you sat at the sewing machine, which was different from the one you had in Split. Although Granddad had oiled it, it was tight and stiff, and felt like no one had ever sewed on it. But you were surprised by the beauty and design of the fabrics in the cupboard in the bedroom of your in-laws, whom you never had the chance to meet. You thought of Charlotte right away, the fabrics could have been French, but they were old and held the scent of lavender. You began to sew yourself dresses, skirts, and slacks. But after a while you realized there was no point to your sewing because you weren't going anywhere where you could deck yourself out like a young bride. You sewed a couple pairs of trousers for Granddad, and for the first time in your life, you also made a number of men's shirts. The garden was beautiful then, too, but you were afraid to sit there, even though inside you felt suffocated by the stale air and the curtains that hung over every window. The two times you took your coffee cup and sat out in the garden with an Italian book pulled from the living room shelves you heard a gunshot. A single shot, but perhaps a fatal one. During the war, you simply never became accustomed to the sound of gunshots and each shot for freedom frightened you even more, upsetting your internal equilibrium; your heart pounded, and you thought it was the end, as though someone were shooting directly at you. After the liberation of Split it was rare to hear a stray bullet; for the most part, there was the quiet of freedom, so valuable that we don't even notice when it's present. But now, here in Castellammare del Golfo, there were bullets coming from you didn't-know-where, or—more importantly—why. Behind locked doors and closed windows...yes, your life moved on behind locked doors, but beyond them you heard the Mafia shootings. This wasn't a novel or a movie but a reality that, evidently, you had not anticipated before moving from Split. A reality of fear, loneliness, and not belonging.

AH, NEDI, what years those were! What troubles Sicily had! Carlo and I were a young married couple, but we lived like old people behind locked doors and closed windows. People came to his cobbler shop downstairs; they knocked for him to come unlock the door, and sometimes when he came upstairs for lunch he was as white as a sheet. He would tell me a name that meant nothing to me, but evidently did to him: there were many Mafiosi in this town, and they were for real. And they wore shoes. Even though they usually bought their shoes in Palermo, when they wanted them polished and sparkling clean, the laces changed, the sole reglued, or their belt fastener fixed, they came to your Granddad, and, even though he had been working as a cobbler for only a few years, he already had experience with these jobs. They would often bring him shoes belonging to their wives, lovers, mothers. What frightened Carlo the most was when they brought a shoe to be repaired and set a pistol on the table next to it. I wanted to be able to peer out from the door and see, but Carlo kept the door leading to the ground floor locked as well. 'A shoe and a pistol,' he would say as if those things came together as a pair. Plus, they usually wanted the work done right there and then. Carlo would try to keep his hand from shaking while the man, waiting for him to glue the sole, took the pistol from the table and spun it between his fingers. 'You don't have any naked women on the walls,' one of them asked him. 'There's nothing for me to look at while I'm waiting.' Carlo went numb with fear. 'I guess you don't need a naked woman on the wall when you've got one of those foreign women upstairs who get undressed faster than ours do,' he laughed in his face. Carlo told me about that one night while we were making love, a time when he was freer than usual. Clearly people in town knew that Carlo had gotten married, to a foreigner no less. I was frightened, too, when Carlo told me. But most of the time he kept quiet about those things, that's the kind of man he was, and more and more it seems to me that he became mute so he wouldn't have to talk any more, it wasn't just from his fear that Margherita could have drowned. Carlo experienced from his Mafiosi customers down in the cobbler shop about everything you could imagine; still, he wasn't struck dumb by their pistols and questions. Despite those things, the two of us truly loved one another. Quietly, a bit old-fashioned, as if we had spent years together, and not several months. The house became more and more a home. I sewed new covers for the pillows and chairs, I used up all the material I had found in the house. When I didn't have anything to sew, I simply read. I hadn't lost my desire to learn. There weren't many books in the house, but those that were there, were interesting and they helped me with my Italian. Carlo and I spoke Italian more and more frequently, and it was only when I couldn't think of a word that I would use the Croatian one and he would pull the word from his memory from his time as a Partisan and he'd understand me. During those first years of our married life, if I don't count the Mafia and my isolation from the outside world, we did, in fact, live peacefully. Then one day I got my period again and I found myself crying. I couldn't get pregnant. I hoped every month, but it somehow didn't happen. I only wrote to Charlotte that we still didn't have a child. I rarely wrote letters to Split and I'm not sure why I didn't feel the need to. Sometimes when my mother wrote to me asking several questions, I only wanted to answer *yes* or *no* in a telegram. And I would laugh at myself: it wasn't for nothing that they called me Non-Oui. Like Carlo, I began to keep quiet, even in writing. Sometimes I caught myself wondering what I was doing here, alone, isolated, with none of my own people, except Carlo. Can a person really live with just one other person, without needing anyone else? Sometimes Anastasia would drop by, but I didn't know what to talk about with her, we were from two different worlds. As for me, I rarely went to see her. You always had to walk through the other house to enter theirs: the passageway between the two houses was strange. Her husband told me that it hadn't been there before, but their neighbor, a member of the Mafia, had simply made the passageway, a sort of atrium between the houses, so he could smuggle drugs. Whenever I passed through there, I trembled with fear thinking someone would grab me from behind and wring my neck. Sometimes Carlo and I managed to go to the little Rosetti store near the upper church to buy everything on the shelves so we would have some reserves. I didn't go to church regularly, only when Carlo thought the little street leading to the church was absolutely safe. Inside the church, the priest always locked the door. Although the sea was right under our noses, we rarely noticed it, and we walked along the shore even more rarely. Carlo, who had so loved catching fish while he lived with me in Split, didn't even think of it now. In this town you had to have a reason and a justification for everything, otherwise trouble could easily find you. There were moments when I missed Split so much, its freedom, my girlfriends, Mama's dinners, and even her inappropriate comments, the fashion catalogues from Charlotte, and that sweet and tragic smile she would make when she called me 'Non-Oui, Non-Oui.' Towards the end of '48 my mother wrote me a strange letter: first, she had neglected to tell me that just after I left, a month after, the Communists in Split had used dynamite to blow up the large nineteenth-century Bajamonti fountain, because Bajamonti had allegedly been an Italian fascist, and there was no room in Socialism for fascist structures. That's what had been announced on the radio. Also, that year, 1948, terrible things were apparently happening in Yugoslavia, there was some sort of Informburo and a political purge taking place and Krsto learned that Yuri had been sent to the prison on Goli Otok island. Apparently, he had said something in defense of the Russians, and, although he was simply young and naïve, he was arrested and sent there along with many other Yugoslavs. As for Vladimir, the father, he gathered up the rest of the family and left Yugoslavia, probably for Russia. In her letter, my mother wondered, 'How could they leave Yuri? Where will he go when he returns from Goli Otok?' His mother hadn't wanted to go, she was born in Split, but Vladimir had always been obstinate. Yuri's grandmother and grandfather had remained in Split. Vladimir always spoke about Croatia as his country, but Russia as his fatherland, even though he had left it in fear and anger. Everyone knew that Russians always believed they would return to Russia, but it rarely happened. But Vladimir did, in fact, return. He said he would take his daughters to safety, he would save them, and he would do whatever he could so that nothing would happen to them like what happened to Yuri and that was all there was to it. My mother also wrote that Krsto had found work as a hauler of baskets of grapes for the 'Vinalko' vineyards and that he came home every day so exhausted that he had settled down a bit and didn't argue with her as he had before. But he didn't have a girlfriend or any friends. 'Not counting the Hajduk fans, but they're his friends only during a match, and then they forget about him.' What could I write back to my mother? I wrote her that everything was fine, that Carlo and I were getting along well, that I was sewing, and that there was nothing else new. I didn't tell her anything about my loneliness, or the fact that I couldn't get pregnant, and even less about the shootings in the street, the locked doors, the closed windows.

FINALLY, IN 1949, Nonna, you gave birth to your first son, my Uncle Mario. 'A miracle!' you told yourself, 'A miracle!' Granddad ran immediately to the small post office with its single wicket and sent a telegram to Split: 'We have a son. Stop. Mario. Stop.

Neda good. Stop.' That's how everyone in Split—not only your mother and Krsto, but through her, your girlfriends and even Charlotte—learned that you had finally given birth to a child, a son, Mario, christened in memory of your mother-in-law Maria, whom you had never met. You were already twenty-six; it didn't matter, what mattered was that you had finally become a mother. Granddad Carlo could barely force himself down to the workshop, he was so preoccupied with the baby. You would sometimes push him downstairs so he would be there, and no one would come to the upstairs door. You always told me that the birth of your son was the greatest achievement of your life. 'Ah, Nedi, a new organ grew inside me when I gave birth to your Uncle Mario. A first child, a new special body part for children': that's what you once told me, do you remember? Two years later you gave birth to my Uncle Luca. He was christened in honour of your father-in-law whom you had also never met. That should have been all it took to give birth. But to give birth in a country with nests of Mafiosi was like stealing eggs from birds. To give birth and to take care of the children in loneliness, in quiet, in limited space, behind locked doors and closed windows, is anything but freedom. But the idea of freedom was no longer clear to you. Your freedom in Split seemed now like a dream, even if it was totally real, and it had been fought for with sacrifice and blood. Whereas here blood flowed for no good reason. 'Out of spite,' Mamma would say. And every time you thought to yourself that in order to have such freedom here in Sicily, Sicily would also have to endure a war. Not something like the Second World War, but a war, nonetheless. Otherwise, it would not be possible for freedom to be won. There was no war, but in the streets of Sicily, and especially in Sicilian homes, battles of life and death often took place.

GRANDMA NEDJELJKA spent the years of motherhood with her children inside, behind locked doors and closed windows. She rarely went out in the yard with them, just enough to breathe a little fresh air. She didn't know herself why she didn't speak Croatian to them rather than her limited Italian since, other than Granddad Carlo, she rarely had the chance to speak with anyone else, usually just a passing conversation at mass with a woman from the neighbourhood or with Anastasia when they saw one another. Her Italian was the language of the books on the shelves in the living room. 'The biggest mistake I made with the children was that I didn't speak to them in Croatian,' she once told me, after she had taught me Croatian, even though she had half-forgotten it by then, or at least that's what she thought. While teaching me Croatian, she even recalled some words in her mother tongue. If she had spoken with Papa and with my uncles in Croatian, maybe she would have felt differently, though still like a foreigner. She would have had something of her own. But she thought that Granddad Carlo wouldn't be happy if she didn't speak to the children in his language. They never talked about it, it was just somehow understood that because she was the foreigner, she should subordinate herself completely to what was expected in her new surroundings.

One day, at Grandma Nedjeljka's insistence, Granddad attached a rope to the small orange tree in the garden so the children could have a swing. Grandma would push them on the swing for just a short time, but then, fearful, she hurried them back into the house after, at most, several minutes even though they wanted to play in the fresh air. It was only when Uncle Mario began school, and Granddad would walk him there, that Mario could take a deep breath of fresh air; he would say, 'at home we don't have any air, we're all going to suffocate.' It was only those years when the children were small and Grandma Nedjeljka spent time with them that her heaviness eased; she was no longer alone, or lonely, even though loneliness is not determined by the number of people and their presence around you, but by your sense that you belong somewhere and that someone belongs to you. Of course, Granddad Carlo had belonged to her the whole time, but the children belonged completely to her, and yet, whether it was because she spoke to them in Italian or because they were boys, she always felt they belonged more to Carlo, than to her. She clearly needed some other support, something like friendship, a confidante. Every person must have another person who knows them to the core. Do I have such a person? Sometimes I think my friend Laura is that person, but I can't count on her all the time, only when she's available. No, my best friend was clearly my Grandma Nedjeljka, no matter how strange that sounds. And when she died, I seemed to get closer to my mother although I was often angry with her because of remarks she had made. Maybe Margherita should have been my best friend, but she was so different from me, she lived only for her meetings with Pietro, something I can't fully understand. If I were in her place, I would have left Pietro by now; I would have found someone else, or I would have resigned myself to my loneliness. It's interesting, even for my girlfriends, their best friends are their mothers. Hmm, that's a new phenomenon for contemporary psychology. Grandma surely missed Charlotte most of all. Even though they didn't see each other that often in Split, every meeting was sincere, meaningful, and warm.

IN OCTOBER 1959 Grandma Nedjeljka received a telegram of just a few words from her mother: 'We need money. Stop. Your father without a grave. Stop.' It was not clear to Grandma Nedjeljka how her father could be without a grave in Split; he was buried in the cemetery in Sustipan sixteen years earlier, in 1943, a few weeks after the Italian capitulation when he was struck by a bullet fired by a random Italian soldier who was swaying drunkenly through the streets of the old town, probably hiding from everyone: the Germans and the locals. It was a sunny autumn day and the soldier, who should have been disarmed already but clearly hadn't been, saw the shadow of a man on the wall of the church and blasted away at the thing drawing near him before he actually saw the man himself. It was Grandma's father, who had finally resolved to join the Partisans, but was shot dead on the spot. The soldier was so frightened that he fled towards the Riva and vanished without a trace. Grandma Nedjeljka was there at the burial, which was one of the last burials of a local resident from Split in that cemetery. It had taken several days of discussions with the city authorities, most of whom were then German rather than people from Split. In the end it was her French teacher who managed to get her father buried there, because Grandma Nedjeljka had once told him during French class that her father loved the islands Šolta, Brač, and Hvar even more than he loved Split and the only place where all three islands were visible was from the graves in Sustipan. Her teacher had also been the one who found her father's body and dragged it home into the yard. She cried inconsolably for her father and, as she told me, no one could calm her; older women dropped by and told her to stop crying, it wasn't nice for a girl her age to cry—it makes them grow old too soon and lose their beauty—but she didn't listen to them. Finally, her mother shouted at her: 'That's enough crying, do you want your father to cry in the next world? If a man like him were to cry he'd be ashamed in front of everyone.' Then Grandma stopped crying, swallowed her tears because of her father's shame and the anger in Krsto's eyes, and that October 1959, when she received the telegram from her mother saying that if she didn't send them money her father would be left without a grave, she pulled from under the heavy starched bedcovers in the bedroom cupboard the bundle of money she had been saving ever since she arrived from Split but had nowhere to spend it in her new home. She said to Granddad, 'Carlo, I'm going to Split, to my father. Look after the children,' and just like that, all by herself, without the children—my Uncle Luca was eight years old then and Uncle Mario ten, my father wasn't born yet—and without her husband, she caught the first bus to Palermo, and from there went by boat to Genoa, then to Ancona, and on to Split where she arrived after nearly a week-long trip. When she arrived in Split everyone was talking about the same thing: the Communists had begun to demolish the graves in Sustipan and people who had money could pay for the bones of their dear departed to be transported to new graves, and those who didn't—they could mourn while the workers tossed the bodies, one atop the other, onto trucks that carried them to a common grave in the new city cemetery. Her mother and brother met her with wonder and disbelief; they thought she would just send the money, not come to Split herself. Her mother kept repeating: 'This is good, this is good, we will save your father,' as if she were talking about a living person whose salvation depended on Grandma Neda's bundle of crumpled bills tucked in her white cotton brassiere. Her brother said nothing; he was still angry at her for marrying Granddad Carlo, his mortal enemy.

AH, NEDI, I set off to Sustipan with my mother and Krsto and with the money, and along the way I saw a red double-decker bus, something we didn't have in Sicily. A London bus! 'Since when were there buses like that driving around Split?' I asked in surprise, for a moment forgetting why we were heading to Sustipan, my brother walking in front, grown-up, but still a misanthrope like he had always been, my mother and I behind him. 'They've been here a few years, there's only a few of them but they drive around all day,' my mother said, quietly, so as not to disturb the sadness weighing on us as we headed to the now-destroyed cemetery. 'But,' I couldn't stop asking questions: 'how did they get them here, what did they bring them on? Can buses that big be transported by boat?' 'Yes, by boat, first to Rijeka—my Rijeka—on a boat named "Romania"—which is strange since the buses came from England, and then from Rijeka to Split by land, along the highway. When all four buses arrived in the city, one after the other, we all went out to see them, as if they had fallen from Mars. What a marvel to behold! You could ride for free for three days. But go try to hop on now, do you know how expensive they are? We still go everywhere on foot, as much as possible.' I wanted to climb on board the bus, but I knew we were heading for Sustipan. There, unbelievable chaos had taken over. Exhumed graves, broken markers, piles of something, most likely bones, wrapped in newspaper, women wailing at the top of their lungs, men arguing with the gravediggers and with the inspectors. It looked like a bomb had gone off in the middle of the cemetery and smashed everything to pieces. We went to the first gravedigger we saw and shoved money into his hand so he would give us our Papa, as we said to him, who was buried in 1943 in the last row of the cemetery. The gravedigger ran ahead of us holding a sheet of paper with the names of the dead and he pointed to ours, stating loudly: 'Mr. Stipe Jagnjić' There, dug up and wrapped in newspaper, was Papa: a little pile of broken bones wrapped in paper propped against a tree right up against the cemetery fence looking towards the city, not the islands that Papa had loved more than Split. I felt his bones inside the paper and shuddered; my brother abruptly pushed me aside so he could lift the bundle, but Mama wrung her hands, crying: 'No, no, not like that, we have to wrap him in something else' and she looked around but there wasn't anything except the green silk scarf I had tied around my neck that morning. She took it from my neck, yanking it with one tug of her hand and I instinctively felt frightened by the pressure on my neck that released as the scarf pulled away. She spread the scarf on the ground, and we gently placed the pile of bones on top, without removing the paper, and then we left on foot, with the scarf tied into a bundle so no bones would fall out, and we carried it to the new city cemetery where we buried him without a priest, without relatives, without friends. This was merely a physical act that we performed, a reburial in a different grave, not a ritual, like when we buried him back in 1943 while down in the city below everyone had already forgotten about Italy's capitulation and young German men marched through the city, their eyes filled with anger.

WHAT DID YOU DO IN SPLIT after that, Nonna? How long did you stay in your old house? Did you go up to your floor? Your brother lives there now, but at that time was your floor still empty? Did you make peace with him? Did you ask whether he knew anything about Yuri, and how long he had been on Goli Otok? Had Yuri come back, where was he? But, apparently, you did not make peace with him, because even unto death you did not speak to one another; he didn't write to you, nor you to him, he had no contact with you, except when your mother died, but he was in a hurry to bury her, so you weren't able to go and see her one more time, even dead, at the ripe old age of 96, still—your mother is your mother. After your first trip, you had fallen ill, first with a cold, then bronchitis, then pneumonia, and you spent two weeks in the hospital in Trapani, and Granddad Carlo and your sons brought you oranges from our tree, and you could barely open your mouth to squeeze a little juice down your throat, you didn't want to eat or drink. Your first trip to Split had left a bitter taste in your mouth.

In Split you had also met your childhood friend, Sonja, at mass at St. Duje's, and she led you outside to tell you that Krunoslav was living in England with a man, and you recalled that after you had reburied your father, and the whole time you felt the absence of the scarf around your neck, your first thought was to go see Charlotte and Marcel. Charlotte had stayed in Split. But Marcel, once he was grown, wanted to leave the place where no one had ever grown accustomed to calling him Marcel, but called him Marko. Marko, the French woman's boy. Though his mother had come to Split way back in 1939, she was still, after twenty years, 'that French woman.' When you went to their house then there was no one there. Locked door, lowered shutters, renovated façade. You knocked on the door, but no one answered. The neighbor woman from the house behind theirs cracked open her window and called out: 'They aren't here, they're in Paris!' That was that. Soon you understood that they were in Paris, but only for the holidays. Everyone would come to Split for the sea, but they traveled the other direction. They headed off to cold Paris, rather than warming themselves in the waters of the Adriatic at Bačvice during that unseasonably warm Split autumn of 1959. 'So Marko could see his relatives in Paris,' added the neighbor, 'Then he'll be coming back to school, he's in the fourth grade.' 'Marko?' you wondered. 'That's what we call him,' the woman laughed. So that's how it was. Charlotte still lived in Split, without a husband, without her mother-in-law who had since died; she decided to remain in the city of her love, sending articles from time to time to French newspapers and magazines, mostly to *Le Monde*. It was enough for a humble life. She didn't let out a room to the increasing number of tourists coming to Split; she didn't want to turn Vid's library into a vacation room, nor the rooms in the basement where they had spent all their days together during the war. 'Out of spite,' Mama would say. Sometimes it's spite that keeps things as they were and how they should remain. For example, the statue of Gregory of Nin that, five years before you arrived for your first visit to Split, was placed opposite the Golden Gate of Diocletian's palace. It was spite—the will to preserve for a full thirteen years the statue's shape, just as your beloved sculptor Ivan Meštrović had given it; it was spite that saved all twenty-seven pieces of the statue which the Italians had tossed outside the old city walls and then reassembled them more than a decade later.

AH NEDI, when I returned from Split and was met by the big hugs of my three boys—that is, your Granddad Carlo who had grown younger along with Mario and Luca—there was nothing I wanted more than to have one more child, nothing more. Although I fell ill, I couldn't stop thinking about it. I felt something had been taken from me in Split: whether it was the grave of my father whom we literally buried in my scarf, or my mother's estrangement, or the hatred I felt from Krsto, whom I no longer hated, at least that's what I thought, or was it Charolotte's absence. And why did Sonja lead me outside the church to tell me that Krunoslav was living in England with a man? I hadn't thought about Krunoslav for years, except when he appeared in my dreams, but I couldn't help that. My other friends had all married and had children older than mine; some had moved away to one place or another, some I no longer recognized. Distance had done its work. I walked through the city, and I was enchanted by each street I recognized, though I rarely saw one that looked the same as it had before the war, still there was an emptiness in me and, it's true, I was like a ghost, just like all people are ghosts once they've left a place; once they no longer live there, it's as if they were dead. I hadn't seen the city for twelve whole years, I hadn't seen my mother for twelve whole years, but when we were left alone in the house, no torrent of words came streaming out of my mouth telling her about my life in Sicily, about Carlo, the children, I was silent and, in my thoughts, I circled back to the time we had spent together, before I left. But it seemed as if the time since I had moved didn't correspond with time in my mother's kitchen, it didn't correspond with her life and Krsto's. Father was no longer anywhere, not in Sustipan, not in our thoughts. Had he begun a new life beyond the grave in the new city cemetery, if it's possible for bones to begin a life? Was he now only a ghost, just like me? I told my mother basic things, but I didn't tell her anything about my loneliness, my fear of the Mafia shootings, about that fact that I didn't speak Croatian with the children. How many language mistakes I made those days in Split! Whenever I needed to say *da*, I would automatically say *si*, and for *ne* I said *no*. It was the same with other words that I used most often: *good, morning, bread* or *time,* I would say them first in Italian. I bought a stack of newspapers and books and that was all I took back with me from Split. Carlo would often joke: 'Not even people with university degrees read as much as you!' Mario and Luca were not pleased with the knit sweaters that their grandma sent for them, but for days on end they sat with shells to their ears and listened to the sea. 'What is your sea called, Mamma?' Luca asked me. 'The Adriatic,' I told him. 'And ours is the Tyrrhenean,' he said. And for a moment I didn't feel either here or there, I didn't belong in Split any longer, and here, in Castellammare del Golfo my own son was telling me that we had different seas. The same with Mario, when he went off to school, he asked me: 'How come in school everyone else has a Sicilian mother, but I have a Yugoslav one?' 'Fate,' I told him, but a snake bit my heart. I was a foreigner; there were only a few of us foreigners in the town! That, at least, would change over the years.

ON MAY 3, 1960 Grandma Nedjejka gave birth to my father, Stefano. She named him herself, after her father, Stipe. In Sicily, there wasn't any name like it, but the Italian version was Stefano. My father, Stefano, is eleven years younger than Uncle Mario and nine years younger than Uncle Luca. Uncle Mario was upset when his mother gave birth to a baby, he said he was too big for crybabies and baby toys, but Uncle Luca happily accepted him and even looked after him while Grandma sewed clothes for all of them. Though she also sewed for a few female customers in town, she had begun to sew mainly for children. Anastasia brought her fashion catalogues from Palermo, and a few times she also got Parisian ones from Charlotte. Her sister would send them to Charlotte from Paris, then Charlotte would send them from Split to my Grandma. Even fashion catalogues had their own travel itineraries. Charlotte was sorry they had missed each other in Split and she wrote to Grandma, 'Who knows whether we will ever see one another again.' Now, with a baby, Grandma didn't want to lose customers, so she sewed whenever there was someone else to watch him. The house was full of males: three sons and a husband. Grandma, at 37 years old, had so much life already behind her and so much still ahead that three times my youthful years would be too few to contain so many memories.

THOUGH, MAYBE NOT. I do have some memories of my own, most of them from the summer I turned eighteen and worked at the small hotel above the bay. Before I had even finished high school in Trapani, Mamma told me that I had to get a summer job; I couldn't just wait for my studies to begin in Palermo. Grandma felt that I should spend my youth as freely as possible, but Mamma just said, 'I'll ask around at church, there must be someone who knows a hotel that needs help.' That same week, after mass, she called to me from the door: 'I'm not even going to take my shoes off. Let's go right now.' 'Where, why?' I asked. 'I found work for you,' she said. And she led me above the bay to the small hotel with green shutters and a small green table out front. I had always loved the way this hotel looked from the outside: there were always interesting tourists sitting there who didn't appear very wealthy, mostly young people who spoke English. The hotel was probably the prettiest in town; the sea in all its blueness and beauty stretched out in front of the hotel. When I was young, my Granddad Carlo and I often went to the harbour and then walked up dozens of stairs to the upper part of town, where before us lay the bay in which Margherita had once almost drowned. One day when I was alone with him, maybe when Margherita was still a baby, Granddad told me a story that I always remembered because he told stories so rarely, though I'm sure he had stories to tell. Many centuries ago, right on that spot, five British boats encircled a Spanish transport ship. The prince of Castellammare del Golfo liked the Spaniards and ordered the British to leave the city. But they began an attack on the small city and people scattered in different directions, pleading, and imploring their saints to protect the city from its enemies. Suddenly, from the hill above the city, the Holy Mother appeared dressed in white with a host of angels moving towards the harbour. The British, frightened by this vision, immediately fled the town. It went something like that. In my memory, I can still see the image of the Madonna, surrounded by angels, storming against the enemies. Sometimes the image seems funny to me—has the Madonna ever stormed anywhere? But that's how Granddad told it to me. Now I was above the harbour and the director of the hotel told me that I could start work immediately; tourists were already starting to arrive, and they needed help with laundry and ironing. But Mamma and I managed to convince her to let me start work after May 15 so I could take care of my marks at school. I would only work afternoons until the school year was over. We were speaking in the hotel restaurant, which was small but pleasant; the pictures on the walls made a particular impression on me: blue sea and blue sky, with the line between them painted as the jagged black lines of an EKG. 'Whose pictures are these?' I asked the director, and she said, 'They're Demetrio's, he's a local artist from San Vito, an older gentleman. He'll be our guest again this year,' she added ruefully, but quickly corrected herself: 'What I meant was that while he was painting these pictures, and ones for the rooms as well, he didn't want payment for the paintings, but wanted instead to spend two weeks a year at the hotel.' And she laughed: 'Maybe we should have insisted on paying him, because it turns out that this is twice as expensive: this is already the fifth year he's been coming and he's a little, how can I put it, odd; he's a bit of a drinker, so he's not exactly the best thing for the hotel's image.' I held myself back from saying that it was probably interesting for the young guests to be able to meet here at the hotel the painter who painted all the paintings in the rooms and the restaurant, even though they were rather kitschy in their blueness, but those black EKG lifelines added an interesting look.

I began working in the hotel after May 15. It was hard work and relations between the employees were terrible. Since I was the youngest worker, they had me doing laundry and ironing; or I'd have to clean the single rooms on the second floor or I'd do the first floor, then back up to the top floor. The chambermaids argued with the director, the director argued with the restaurant supplier, the driver argued with the workers who arrived to fix a faucet or a sink. It felt like everyone was arguing with everyone. There was a woman working in the ironing room; everyone thought she was crazy and no one talked to her; the director told me that I didn't need to talk with her either. 'Leave her alone, she's crazy, I gave her work because the social agency pushed me into it, every institution has to employ someone with special needs. This one just needs sex, that's all, look how she's dressed.' The woman, who was wearing a see-through t-shirt displaying a worn-out bra, was named Liza; she was fifty years old, and had, evidently, been a beauty in her youth. She said she had even studied languages and literature at the University in Palermo, but fate intervened, and now she found herself here in the ironing room of the hotel. 'She was married, had a daughter; they lived in Palermo; one night the building caught fire. They lived on the ground floor—they were subletting. Everything started to burn, but she just sat on the balcony smoking her last cigarette; she was a smoking fiend, then when the fire flared up, she couldn't get back inside; there was nothing for her to do but jump, so she instinctively jumped and nothing happened to her, it was low to the ground and she ran through the entrance to the apartment to save her daughter and husband, but they were already dead. Some people say the Mafia set the fire to kill someone in the building, others said it was an electrical fire.' That's what I heard from the oldest chambermaid, who was apparently a friend of Liza's when Liza came to work in the hotel, but they fought over some trivial things and Liza no longer wanted to see her, let alone talk to her. This Liza saw me, the youngest, and somehow drew close to me; she helped me iron with the big ironing machine, helped me take the sheets from the washing machines, and when I was on a floor cleaning the rooms, she would appear and run the vacuum cleaner in some rooms or clean some the toilet bowls for me—she was like my angel helper. Until Demetrio, the creator of the paintings, came. He was a fifty-year old, bearded man with oily black hair, an energetic man who immediately got to know all the new employees. He looked Liza right in her eyes and said: 'That's too skinny a body for a person like the one hiding in your eyes,' then to me, he said: 'What's your name? Neda? Where did you ever come up with a name like that? I'm going to call you Piccola.' Then, while we worked and the guests enjoyed themselves, swimming, taking strolls, and casually eating out on the green tables out in front of the hotel, Demetrio sat on the balcony making remarks about one or another of them. He'd often call out to tell some of the guests that he wanted to sketch them. They enjoyed it, plus they didn't pay for the portraits. One day he said he wanted to draw me, too. 'Piccola,' he said to me, 'will you ask your father, or will you decide for yourself if I can draw you?' 'I'll decide myself,' I laughed and let him draw my portrait; I had to sit a whole hour beneath his balcony looking up. It would have been more pleasant with my eyes closed, like sunbathing, but with eyes open it was torture. It was a good thing the director of the hotel wasn't around; she went home every afternoon, so I could sit there doing nothing until the sketch was done. Liza whispered to me: 'He drew me, too.' I could see that Liza liked to be around him, she found ways to be beneath his balcony when he was there, or she would leave the ironing room and go to the small restaurant while he was eating lunch. I've always found it interesting watching grownups, to see how they react in specific situations, what sort of relations develop between them, to hear the conversations of other people. That's why I liked listening to Grandma Nedjeljka telling me stories about her life. Still, in the hotel, I was witness to all sorts of things: once, while I was cleaning the hallway with double rooms on the ground floor, I heard a man talking to his wife—or whoever the woman in the room was; the door was open and from the hallway all that was visible were their bare feet on the bed: I heard him tell her that when he was a child on vacation with his parents, one day he was wearing yellow swimming trunks and a blue cap. He was sitting in the lounge chair on the beach eating an apple while his father, who was still in love with his mother—he said that 'still' in a different tone of voice—ran his hands down her sides, and the two of them were laughing. They laughed the whole day, about this and that, about sexual things he hadn't understood then. At night they made love. From his spare bed by the balcony door, he saw the two of them get up from their beds, go to the bathroom, and once inside they moaned and groaned, his mother even shouted several times. Every night, and during the day, while he pretended to be asleep, they kissed one another, rolled around in the bed, then went into the bathroom, while he, he told her, held his penis so it wouldn't fly out of his underpants. Then a strong draft, or his parents, would shut the door to the room. Even today I remember those yellow swimming trunks.

At least there weren't tense relations among the guests as there were among the employees, especially between the director and everyone else, but also between everyone and everyone. It seems that only Liza, deep in her own world of sedatives and misfortunes, had no need for tense relations with others, really, she had no need of any relations with anyone, except Demetrio, and me. It wasn't clear to me when and how they became a couple or whether they just slept together, but Demetrio often came out of her room. Then, after a few days, we all heard him slam the door and shout: 'I'm not coming here anymore, you know! I told you to move them, but you want it your way, so let someone else fuck you.' Liza wasn't any more unhappy now than she had been before: when your child and husband have died in a catastrophe, no other troubles can touch you. Romantic troubles even less. I hadn't intended to peek in her room, but one day, the door was open, so I stepped part way in. Everything was just like all the single hotel rooms, where she was allowed to live on account of her 'delicate' condition, as the director said, while all the other chambermaids, cooks, and cleaners who did not live in Castellammare del Golfo were housed in rooms with four beds up in the attic. The director even ordered a few more beds to be dragged up there so there would be space for everybody: most of the employees were from the far reaches of Sicily, I was one of the rare few who went home after work. But Liza's bed drew my attention: there were a number of objects, little things, lined up along the wall, one beside the other, like in an exhibit: a straw bear with a blackened head that was missing an arm, a bundle of keys, a white-dotted blue milk cup that was completely charred on one side, a gold ring on a thread hanging from a nail at the same height as the other objects, a blackened doll leg, a broken shaving mirror, plus a few other things I couldn't recognize. The pillow on the bed didn't have the usual hotel white pillowcase with lace trim but was stuffed into a child's dress trimmed with ribbons, the short sleeves hanging to the sides. I nearly fainted when I saw all of this. It was then I understood that Liza was, in fact, not normal; she was different from the normal people I knew; after that fateful fire, she had searched through the ruins of the building to find these reminders of her family life; and I understood that her personal tragedy was so much more than a collection of facts about someone who works with you in the same hotel.

I turned eighteen on June 7 that year. I was working the second shift and I brought some of the Split cake that Grandma had made especially for the occasion. When we finished work for the day, we sat around the employees' table and everyone wished me luck, though I didn't blow out any candles. Even the cook said she had never tasted a more delicious cake in her life. Unfortunately, I didn't have enough for the guests in the hotel. Demetrio showed up with a guitar. He began to play and sing old Sicilian songs. I remembered when Grandma told me about her brother and the Russian boy going to see Granddad Carlo at the headquarters to sing Dalmatian and Russian songs, and he got angry because they didn't know a single Sicilian one. Grandpa started singing one himself before he broke Krsto's finger. I had a feeling that Demetrio was singing that same song. He continued singing and playing for a long time, after nearly everyone had gone, even several of the guests who had been sitting in the foyer between the kitchen and the restaurant reserved for us employees. I didn't feel comfortable leaving because I was the one celebrating and I wanted at least someone to stay, even Liza, but Liza was the first to go since she and Demetrio had had a total falling out. Somewhere around midnight Demetrio stopped playing, got up, kissed me on the forehead and said: 'Now go home. As of tomorrow, you are full grown, and you can choose for yourself whether to go or not.' I got up and went home. The next day, they told me Demetrio had left. To the director, he told her: 'I think over these several years you've already paid for the pictures I painted. Don't expect me again next year.'

I didn't want them to expect me the next year either. I worked till the very end of the summer and then in the fall, with the money I had earned, I bought myself a year's bus ticket for the route Castellammare del Golfo—Palermo and I began my studies in Culture and Society, regularly traveling an hour and a half there and an hour and a half back. The ticket, though, was at a reduced rate since I was the child of an employee of the Ruso bus company, though Papà didn't drive buses, only minibuses, so I never traveled with him to Palermo and back.

January 1968, Split—Castellammare del Golfo

GRANDMA ONCE SAID TO ME when I asked her to tell me about her second trip to Split, her first with her sons: 'Ah, Nedi, my French teacher would tell us that there are personal memories and collective memories. But I know there is not a single person or country that doesn't remember '68. It is the month of January that year that really stays in my memory.' When Papà was eight years old, Uncle Luca seventeen, and Uncle Mario nineteen, Granddad Carlo told Grandma approvingly to take them all to Split, chiding her with a gentle tone: 'It's about time, maybe it's even already past the time, you should take them there!' Granddad Carlo didn't want to go, for him Split, as a geographic location, only existed until his departure in 1945, right after the incident in Sustipan with Grandma's brother. In fact, if Uncle Luca and Uncle Mario hadn't already been so old when they first went to Split, if they hadn't begged their mother to take them to the place she came from so they could see for themselves the Split she had been talking incessantly about for years, this Spalato, as everyone called it but Grandma and me, if my uncles and Papà hadn't worn her out asking about this trip, who knows whether Grandma would ever have seen Split again. I never understood that—your whole life you talk about a city, about your home town, you long for it and dream about it, but you're not able to go there, you can't bridge the physical distance to find yourself again in the narrow streets you still know from memory, to be again on that unforgettable Riva where you locked eyes with Granddad Carlo, to climb once again the mountain called *Marjan* where perhaps the red or tricolour flag still flies, to peek into the gardens of your relatives and friends, most of whom have either moved around the globe or off into the heavens. To wish to return for at least a moment to the place you came from, but not have a speck of courage to make that return trip. After Grandma's sudden, strange trip in 1959, all alone, with money hidden in her brassiere to exhume her father's bones, Grandma Nedjeljka had made peace with the fact that she would not see her native land again. But now, with the children growing up, all boys, at that, her only worry was that they didn't know Croatian—though in some way she was also relieved, thinking how her brother could insult them—she felt stronger about such a trip, stronger even to face Krsto who now lived in the house, on 'her floor' with his family: his wife Vesna, a Serbian woman whom he had met during a volunteer work action in 1964 when the Adriatic highway was being built, and their three-year old daughter, Marina. Grandma hoped that her brother, although he had not written a single word to her during these years, would have changed for the better, since, with a wife and child, a person should become a better person, kinder, more grateful, even if they are older when they finally establish a family. There were still two bedrooms below, on the ground floor, so it wouldn't be a problem finding room to stay. After ushering in New Year's 1968, they set off for Split, having sent a telegram addressed to her mother: 'We are coming. Stop. Me and the children. Stop.' Traveling by boat, bus, train, and boat again, they arrived in Split the evening before Epiphany. Exhausted from the travel, they all just stared into space as they sat around the kitchen table while Grandma's mother, now quite old and worn down, barely dragged herself from stove to sink to bring to the table plates of olives, cheese, and prosciutto, and to pour the rosemary tea, but she couldn't cut the bread, as the knife seemed to slip from her fingers, but Uncle Mario took it and cut two slices of bread for himself and for everyone else. The boys said nothing, but Grandma simply said: 'Don't Mama, stop. This is enough, Mama. You don't need to slice anymore. We all have some, Mama.'

AH NEDI, is that what it's like in all families that haven't seen one another for so many years? You sit, and you realize that your place isn't there, it's as if you're sitting in someone else's place. The children sat there, eating silently; your Uncle Mario was already a man, Luca too, and I didn't know what else to say to my mother, other than to tell her not to put more food on the table. From the look on her face, I couldn't tell whether she was happy we had come or whether it was all too much for her. She looked most at Mario, I think his eyes reminded her of Carlo, but she said nothing to me. For the first time, I noticed that one of her legs was lame, just like one of Papà's. Something must have happened to her, but how could I ask when I hadn't seen her for a full nine years? I looked around, seeking a trace of myself in the kitchen. And there, behind the glass of the kitchen cupboard stood an old photograph of us: your father, still a baby, Mario, and Luca hugging me around the waist. Carlo wasn't in the photo; he had taken it. I remember the moment when the polaroid photo came out of the camera and Carlo told me that he would put it in an envelope, and he would send it to my mother himself. But as for anything else that could serve as a reminder that I had once lived in this house—there was nothing. I gathered my strength and asked my mother how Krsto was, and where he was. She only looked up and said: 'He'll come down; he's probably putting Marina to bed. His wife is making her special Christmas bread. We're celebrating Epiphany, but they have their Christmas, and there you have it. Ever since he married a Serb.' It hadn't occurred to me that for us Catholics it was Epiphany, but for the Orthodox it was Christmas. With two holidays in the house, the atmosphere was tense and troubled. My mother didn't know what to do with the children, especially Mario, who was nearly a man, not a boy. It was the first time I felt ashamed that I hadn't taught them Croatian. After we had sat a whole hour at the table trying to talk about something, anything, Krsto and his wife came down to the kitchen. She might have been a bit younger than he was, but, still, she wasn't any younger than thirty. It seemed that the two of them had found one another during the work action at a time when they both thought they'd never in their lives find a soulmate. As if Krsto could even have a soulmate! Krsto looked sullen, but nonetheless managed to say: 'The Mafiosi have arrived,' and a smile played at the edges of his mouth as the children stood, as if by command, and extended a hand to him. Vesna, however, smiling, made-up, dressed as if for the Corzo, greeted us warmly, as if we had known one another for years. 'What's it like raising children surrounded by Mafia?' she asked me. 'We manage,' I said. 'Life with three sons and a husband spins faster than the Mafia escapades, even in Sicily,' and I smiled. We exchanged a few remarks about this and that, Vesna boasted that they had gas lamps installed, and she joked that unlike them, she knew both Croatian and Serbian, then she quickly excused herself saying she had to go upstairs in case Marina woke and started crying.

Krsto stayed, however. And, as soon as his wife went upstairs to their upper floor, he turned to Grandma—who couldn't help staring at his left hand to see if his little finger still dangled, and indeed, it did, even so many years after the incident with Carlo—and asked in a sharp tone whether she had kept the small bone from their father's remains from the time they collected his bones and carried them in her scarf to the other city cemetery. 'What small bone, what are you talking about, I don't have any sort of bone,' Grandma answered but he didn't believe her. 'It has to have been in your hand, you just won't admit it. You were a bitch and a bitch you've remained,' he said to her, and it was a good thing that my Papà and uncles didn't understand Croatian because anything could have happened. Their Grandma just crossed herself and said quietly to Krsto: 'Go on, son, don't keep Vesna waiting for you upstairs, it's a holiday.'

They celebrated Epiphany mass at Saint Mary's then at home Grandma Nedjeljka roasted pork and potatoes. Her mother made special Dalmatian doughnuts, and they put everything on the table that was then available in the market. Krsto and his family didn't eat with them, but towards evening Vesna brought a whole plate of the foods she had prepared for her Orthodox Christmas. The different foods intermingled on the table, but Krsto didn't come down. No one even thought about him, however, since the centre of attention was Marina, his three-year old curly-haired daughter, who was Papà's and his brothers' first cousin. Grandma, like a true aunt coming from abroad, had bought for her in Palermo the largest and most beautiful doll she could find, one with a crying mechanism. But Marina was frightened by the crying doll and just looked at it, then didn't dare touch it again. Not even Papà knew what to play with her, even though he was the youngest and closest to her age. They looked at her, laughed with her, tickled her, pinched her cheeks, and Uncle Mario made animal faces for her. Grandma felt some warmth in the house for the first time, but Vesna didn't dare invite them upstairs, up to their floor even though what she wanted most of all was to see 'her' floor, where she had spent the best, and the worst, days of her youth.

AH, NEDI, I kept telling myself the whole time: why did I need to come, why did I bring the children; when you don't live in a place it means you're dead there. It's only in the next world that a dead person can travel where he was once alive. We had round-trip tickets, with a return on January 16th. That's what Carlo got for us. He said we needed to stay at least ten days in Split, so we could see everyone. But who would we see? I didn't even think about looking for my old girlfriends; who knew whether they were still alive, or whether they still lived in Split? I knew that Yulia had moved to Australia. I just couldn't bring myself to knock on one of the doors from the past and have someone I didn't know answer. But, right after the holiday, I went to Dobri to Charlotte's. I thought I would see her, and give her a hug, and she would say to me, like always: 'Non-Oui, Non-Oui.' In fact, I hadn't had any news of her since 1959 when, after my first trip to Split, I had written her a long letter, and she answered that she had, indeed, been with Marcel in Paris, but when they returned to Split, Marcel said he didn't want to stay there, he wanted to return to Paris, with her or without her, and so, just like that, they sold the house for not that much money and returned to Paris. Marcel planned to finish high school in Paris and then study art, maybe photography. She also said that she didn't know whether we would ever see one another again. She never contacted me again, and I didn't have her address in Paris. Still, I wanted to go to the house where they had lived, maybe someone there could tell me more. There was no one in the house, it looked abandoned or like those sea-side houses that are full only during the summer, and during the other months languish in their loneliness. I had the feeling that no one I had known still lived in Split. I thought about Yuri, and the fact that he died on Goli Otok, at least that's what the talk was on the Riva, that he was left there to his fate and that he died beneath a rock that slipped and fell directly on top of him while he was climbing in the quarry. 'Russian fatalism, I tell you, I've been to school, I know what that is,' a witness said. Quite different from his family's hope that they would find peace in Russia. 'Mama, you don't know anyone here,' Mario said to me as we were walking along the Riva. 'No one knows me anymore,' I said to him, since I did recognize a few people, like the pharmacist on Marmontova Street or the priest at St. Duje's, or the vegetable-seller at the market stall next to the one my mother had when I was a child. But they no longer recognized me, because I tell you, a person who doesn't live in a place is dead and can only come back as a ghost, but who likes ghosts? The only thing that stays the same is the sea, nothing else, it is unchangeable, the same colour, the same sounds, the same quiet.

ON JANUARY 11 outside on the street they heard voices and the pounding of footsteps. It seemed like everyone was heading in the same direction; people were racing along the streets towards the palace, and, inside the palace walls, along the narrow streets heading to the Peristile, the palace castle. 'What's going on?' Grandma Nedjeljka asked her mother who was standing in the doorway watching the people running past. 'Something in the Peristile, who knows...' she said and closed the door. But Grandma gathered the children and they set off with rapid steps into the mass of people. When they made their way through the streets to the palace and reached the Peristile, they, like everyone else, stood stock still, shocked by what awaited them. The Peristile had been painted entirely red. It looked like blood had been spilled during the night, the entire small square within Diocletian's palace was covered in paint, something Grandma had never seen before in her life. Like all the others, she was afraid that something awful, some terrible deed, had taken place during the night. But soon voices could be heard saying that some students had poured the thirty litres of paint that they had been buying from the paint and varnish store, one can at a time so as not to raise any suspicions. The next day, their names were known, they were arrested, and locked up for a few hours in a gallery space, then they had to clean the paint from the castle courtyard. The newspapers called it an act of vandalism, and the artists, because that's what they were, vandals. Later when I read about the Red Peristile I understood that it had, in fact, been an act to express their dissatisfaction with the artistic and political scene in Split, in Croatia, and in all of Yugoslavia, that this act of protest had been in the spirit of other protests that had gripped Europe and America in 1968. And, most tragically of all, several members of the group committed suicide a short time after the event, one of them simply jumped from the thirteenth floor of the skyscraper in Split with a sign around his neck stating: 'I am an artist,' in a performance piece entitled 'I am an artist.' But for

Grandma, the red Peristile jolted her from her normal life axis: she understood that Split could get along without anyone, that there would always be someone who would momentarily make his mark, and then have to erase that mark himself. How had she marked Split? By the uniforms she had sewed for the Partisans? But did anyone even know that she had sewn them with her aunt? Was it the dresses that she had sewn after the war? Or the fact that she had brought Granddad Carlo into her home? Or by the fact that she had been excluded from WAF after that hasty ruling against her, without due process? Or the fact that she wore a red beret both when Italy capitulated on September 8, 1943 and on 26 October 1945, the first anniversary of the liberation of the city? It was by all those things, and by nothing. She had erased herself from the city when she left.

AH, NEDI, the day after that event, I went directly to Vesna and begged her to allow me to see the upper floor of the house. 'I would have invited you up myself,' she said to me, 'But Krsto...' Fortunately, he was at work, so I went up with the children. Marina clapped her little hands when she saw us, and I went straight to the room where the sewing machine had been. And just think—the sewing machine was still there. The bed was new, and so were the cupboards, but the sewing machine was still standing. It was the only thing remaining from my aunt and my uncle. 'I sew a few things for the house,' Vesna said as if excusing herself. 'That's fine,' I said, 'that's what a sewing machine is for.' I automatically opened the little door in the cupboard, but Vesna said to me: 'I threw everything away that was in there, there were a lot of moths inside.' So that's how it was, moths had even eaten the cloth eyes I had made after my first meeting with Carlo, and Krunoslav's poems. Banality can destroy those things we thought would last forever.

Nearly everything had been changed in the other rooms as well, but a few things were still there: three of the small pillows that I hadn't taken to Sicily as part of my trousseau, two old photographs on the walls, a wooden chair I had rested my feet on when I had to sew something by hand. I was both present and not present on 'my' floor. There was a television now, while my mother only had a radio downstairs. The children were captivated by the television, and they wanted to stay to watch something, and I told Vesna they could stay until Krsto got back from work; they stayed, but Mario and Luca soon came downstairs saying they were too big for such children's shows and they were going out for a walk around town. They were, in fact, too big for such things, but they had no friends to go out with in Split; they simply wanted us to go home as soon as possible and, to tell the truth, I could barely wait for January 16 so we could return to Sicily.

BUT DURING THE EVENING OF JANUARY 14TH, Vesna tumbled downstairs into the kitchen, shouting: 'Have you heard? There was an earthquake in Sicily, a lot of people are dead. Trepani, Trapani, or something like that.' Krsto came down right after her with Marina in his arms. 'Turn on the radio,' he told our mother. On the radio they announced that a large earthquake had occurred in the Trapani region, but, fortunately, they didn't mention Castellammare del Golfo. They only mentioned Gibellina and Salaparuta, which had been flattened to the ground. There were hundreds dead and missing. 'What about Carlo?' your mother asked. 'Carlo is in Castellammare, he doesn't drive the minibus at night,' said Grandma, her heart pounding in her temples, unable to catch her breath. Papà barely understood what was happening, Grandma translated for him what she had heard and everyone else was nearly faint by all the news. 'Could Papà have been driving there?' Luca asked, but Grandma had heard distinctly that the earthquake took place at night, or in the early morning hours when Carlo was not at work. They mentioned Belize and a few other places, but not a word about Castellammare del Golfo. 'Sicily is a cursed place, the Mafia even causes earthquakes,' muttered Krsto. 'What is he saying?' Uncle Mario turned to his mother. 'That the Mafia even causes earthquakes in Sicily,' she translated for him as quietly as possible. She didn't close an eye until the morning they were to depart for Sicily. Uncle Mario slept with clenched fists and in the morning when he awoke, the palms of his hands were blue and his fingers numb.

ACCORDING TO GRANDMA, from that point on Uncle Mario wanted to move away from Castellammare and away from Sicily. He couldn't bear the Mafia past or the Mafia present on the island, nor the thought that tectonic shifts had leveled two cities near Castellammare del Golfo. Plus, he didn't feel particularly good about the fact that it was surrounded on all sides by water, like a sinking ship. So, he moved to Trieste to study architecture. A while after he met Antonia, who was also nearing the end of her studies; they fell in love and quickly got married in a church there and told the family at home after the fact. Granddad was very offended, but Grandma tried to understand them. 'Our marriage was like that, too,' she told Carlo, 'it was quick as lightening—do you remember how the priest locked us in the church?' 'Yes, but the first-born son should be married in the right way,' he said. But everyone forgot about all that when the young bride died in childbirth a few months later, for no apparent reason, as the doctors said; she gave birth, closed her eyes, and did not wake up again. They named the child Antonio after his mother. The shock of Antonia's death was so great that Mario caught the first boat for Sicily and came home, while the baby was still in the hospital. Social services took care of it, but Grandma always said that the Lord alone had saved Antonio from ending up in someone else's family during the time Mario simply stayed at home with his parents, sitting in silence, without the strength even to cry. After several months someone contacted him from Trieste: did he want the child, or should it be given to someone? He returned, took the child, hired a woman to help him, and did not want Grandma and Granddad to go to be with him. 'You need to take care of Stefano,' he told them. Uncle Mario somehow pulled through. Children grow quickly. When Antonio was five years old, the architecture firm where Uncle Mario worked hired Alessandra, his current wife. He liked her, and she him. At their first date after work, he told her his fate. And she told him hers: while she was pregnant with her son Marco, her husband died. Young, only 30-years old, a heart attack. Marco was born the same year as Antonio. 'They could almost have been twins, with different mothers,' Uncle Mario tried to laugh. There was no way then to go back: Alessandra soon moved in with Uncle Mario together with Marco, and the two five-year-old's became brothers, whether they liked it or not. That's why, through one uncle, I have two cousins from two different mothers, two different aunts.

AH, NEDI, three years later, Uncle Luca married Mirela. He had already been living for ten years in Rome, where he had gone to study law. When he was young, he always said, 'When I grow up, I'm going to become a judge and I'll convict the Mafioso who killed Grandma!' Then, after he completed international law in Rome, he no longer wanted to come back to Castellammare. He didn't become a judge, but a lawyer. And since he was always justice-loving and honourable, he agreed to work pro bono one day a week in the law office where he worked. Free legal help, something like that. For immigrants, homeless people, anyone who needed legal advice but couldn't afford to pay for it. One day, he wrote to us from Rome that he had found a beautiful and educated girl—a woman—that's what he wrote, and it wasn't clear to your Granddad Carlo or to me what he meant by that, and also that she was a Romanian named Mirela, who had moved to Rome, and they would get married right after Epiphany. They would be having only a small celebration, and nothing else, but all of us should come, and he also invited Mario with his family. 'So, Luca is also marrying a foreigner,' your Granddad Carlo said, and I didn't know whether to take that as something good or bad. It wasn't really like him to say something like that. I have to admit, the thought did pop into my head for a moment: 'what, he couldn't find an Italian, so he's marrying a Romanian?' In Sicily, we had only heard bad things about Romanians, nothing else, things like the majority of them were dying from hunger unless they were close to Ceaușescu, then they lived like gods in palaces. And now all of a sudden– some Mirela or other from Romania—would become our daughter-in-law. I'm telling you this so you'll know that a person who was an outsider, a foreigner, can, for a moment, think that a native-born is better than a newcomer, especially in the case of women. After all, isn't it usually the women who relocate? You're educated, surely something like that's been written in books. In any case, my resistance to the idea quickly passed and, thank God, Luca never found out that such a thought had crossed my mind. You know yourself how kind he is. We all got ready to go to Rome, your granddad went off to see about tickets and the best way to get to Rome, we had even already bought presents, but all roads do not always lead to Rome, and our plans were interrupted by the Mafia, what else. Castellammare will, if for no other reason, be remembered in history as the town with the most Mafiosi. One of them had killed Piersanti Mattarella in Palermo. The president of the Regional Government of Sicily. On Epiphany, on a holiday, as he was driving with his wife and children to mass! At first, people said it was the neo-Fascists that killed him and his family, but then people learned that the Mafia assassinated him because he was working too hard to step on their fingers. Apparently, he wanted to stamp out violence in the construction branch of the Mafia, the Cosa Nostra, and to prevent construction companies from having to pay rackets and bribes, so construction could develop like in the rest of Italy. But it's the honourable people and revolutionaries that get killed, right? The news immediately spread through the town and at first no one knew whether the president was the only one killed or whether his wife and children were as well. It was confirmed that the killer was from here and that he was probably here and in hiding. The municipal authorities shut down all the bus and boat lines and set up blockades at the exit from town. No one could get in or out. So how could we go to Rome? No how! Even though the police knew Carlo—he fixed their shoes, too—they told him it was for his own good to stay home until the situation was resolved, especially since we would have to travel first to

Palermo and then to Rome. Everyone from Castellammare del Golfo would be inspected in Rome, held for interrogation in the police department and, most likely, sent back. And then what? So, we stayed home. Disappointed, angry, sad. Your Uncle Luca even more, the poor thing.

HE AND MIRELA were married alone, without either his family or hers since they were back in Romania. It was only when they came here a half year later, during the summer, that Grandma, Granddad, and Papà could give them their presents and become acquainted with Mirela. Mirela was, indeed, no girl, but a woman. She was five years older than Uncle Luca. She had been an English teacher in a Bucharest high school. Because she knew English, she was under constant observation by the Security Forces. Everything was fine, pretty much in order, until the day she read Ginsberg's poem 'America' to the students. This was forbidden literature in high school. One of the students, whose father was in the upper echelons of Ceauşescu's government, informed on her. She was dismissed from work that same day. She had been married for six months. Some of her friends told her that the Security Forces wouldn't leave it at just dismissing her from work, she would be punished in some other way for introducing American propaganda in the high school. It would be best if she left the country. Her husband didn't want to leave but did everything so she could. Did he not love her enough, or did he love her too much? Who knows? What's important is that he submitted divorce papers, which was taken as a moral act on his part, then he swam with her half-way across the Danube, swam back, and waited hidden in the tall rushes in the river to see that she made it all the way across. She probably never imagined herself that she could swim across such a river. When it's a matter of life or death, a person gives himself over to God and leaves it in his hands whether they'll sink or swim. Some people in Yugoslavia helped her. From there she took a train for Trieste and on to Rome. And there, without means and without documents she found herself in the Centre for Foreigners. They sent her to Uncle Luca for legal help. She told him she was an English teacher, but that in Italy she would do any sort of work, if he'd just help her. She could tell fortunes by reading coffee grounds, as her mother had taught her when she was still a child. And she was so insistent on reading his fortune that, at their third meeting, they had a coffee together and that's how it all started. She had seen herself in his cup, but only told him that a life with a foreigner awaited him. As for Uncle Luca, with his noble heart, he couldn't help falling in love with her.

NONNA, wasn't it a good thing that, for a few years at least, Mirela was part of our family, and you weren't the only new-comer and foreigner? Unfortunately, Aunt Mirela, whom I never met, despite how lucky she had been, couldn't have children. In that cold water of the Danube her ovaries had given up forever. Then, after 1989 when Ceaușescu was killed, she went to Romania with a suitcase full of money to adopt a child, she wanted it to be Romanian so she could have someone to talk with in her own language, and she never returned. She wrote to Uncle Luca that she had adopted a child, but she wasn't planning to return to Rome. Simply put: when she entered Romania, she felt like she was coming home. Forever. She would always be grateful to him for his wonderful gift. You cried so much, didn't you? Poor Uncle Luca, so good, and so alone. It's good that at least my Papà brought home a pretty normal daughter-in-law, so long as we don't count that saying of hers 'Out of spite,' right?

OUT OF SPITE OR NOT, on June 7, 1988 I was born. Stefano's first daughter and a first granddaughter for Granddad Carlo and Grandma Nedjeljka. My father wanted to honour her and so, as the first granddaughter, they christened me with her name. My mother told me from the time I was little that she had made the biggest mistake in her life when she had given in to Papà because she now understood that because of that name I'd never find a husband; after all, in Sicily who wants a wife called Nedjeljka, and that's why I still haven't brought a young man home. 'Then why did Granddad marry a woman with that name?' I asked her. 'Well, because...' Maybe it's not the name but my choosiness that's at fault. What was it that Grandma Nedjeljka, a seamstress, taught me? She said: 'If you see a white thread—you'll find a blond-haired boy, if you see a black one—a black-haired one, if you see a brown thread—a boy with chestnut brown hair.' 'And what if I see a thread in a different colour?' I'd ask. 'Well red means a Communist, pink a capitalist, and blue—a foreigner.' 'How do you know that blue means a foreigner?' I asked her. 'Because the sea and the sky are blue, and the only creatures moving across the sea and the sky are creatures with no home, foreigners.' But I didn't notice a single thread on any of the young men I met. But maybe I just couldn't recognize it—you can't see a black thread on black fabric, or white on white.

And, my name Nedjeljka is hard to say in Italian, it ties up your tongue and, rather than the soft *l* sound, some strange *l* comes out. Most people call me Neda, just like they called Grandma. Whenever I meet Italians who don't live in Sicily, but come here to vacation on 'this pile of land' as they jokingly call it, and I tell them my name, their reaction is always the same, they smirk and ask: 'Are you an immigrant?' 'No, no I was born in Castellammare.' The faces of the people I'm talking to relax into a smile and there's a kind of ease—she's one of us! But some continue: 'Then what kind of name is Nedelka?' 'Nedjeljka,' I correct them, softening the *l*-sounds, 'In Italian it means Domenica, Nedela.' But, in what language?' 'In Croatian.' 'A Croatian name in Sicily?!' they are amazed and some then add: 'You must have been born on a Sunday.' Then I begin to laugh, 'No, no. I was born on a Wednesday, but I was christened with my grandmother's name, she was named Nedjeljka and she was from Split, from Spalato, Croatia.' 'Yugoslavia,' they nod.

As for the foreigners—especially the young people who often gathered at the bay and seduced the girls from town, just as we often did them—they would laugh like crazy when I told them my name. 'You must have whacky parents,' they responded. 'No, I had that kind of Grandma,' I tell them, and I know that Grandma Nedjeljka wouldn't be insulted, but would agree that that was the case. One guy, writing on Trip Advisor about Castellammare del Golfo wrote that the sea was beautiful, the town gorgeous, but the church bells rang too loudly, and a girl he liked, maybe a daughter of some Mafioso in the town with Balkan roots, had an unfortunate name that made it too hard to get to know her well. I didn't even know who wrote it but there are all kinds of tourists in the world. And, in Italy, or in Sicily, at least, I am sure I am one of the rare, if not the only, Nedjeljka.

Before they had me, my grandparents first grandchild was my cousin Antonio, Uncle Mario's son, but no one would possibly have considered giving him the name Nedjeljko or Carlo, since the most normal thing was for him to carry the name of his poor mother who had died in childbirth. Grandma and Granddad also loved Marco, but never as their grandson, I think, but more like a guest, and he rarely came to our place in Castellammare del Golfo. And when Margherita was born, my mother, while she was still in the labour room, wrote the name herself on the birth certificate in the crib and presented Papà with a *fait accompli*, and it didn't even occur to him to insist on her being named Carla. Still, Margherita never quite understood whether she was named Margherita for Mamma's favourite pizza, or for Margaret Thatcher, who was Mamma's idol, or for some other reason. In any case, no one asked Margherita why she was named that. But everyone asked me, and some people wanted to call me Domenica, but I never allowed it: either Nedjeljka, or Neda, or nothing. It's true that my mother never learned how to say Nedjeljka correctly, so she always called me Neda, but Grandma always called me Nedi, and if Papà didn't call me Nedjeljka, I wouldn't even know that that's what my name really is. At school, all the children were called by their full names, but I was called by my nickname, Neda, not because I was so beloved in my class, but because it was easier. Still, I called my Grandma 'Nonna Nedjeljka' like she wanted me to, or 'Grandma Non-Oui' as she was called in Split, a place where, as Grandma would say, people always spoke a bit differently, their vowels in Dalmatian dialect slightly different than in other dialects. 'And in French,' I would always add.

SEVERAL MONTHS after Granddad Carlo died, the morning that Grandma Nedjeljka was supposed to go to Split, she said to me: Ah, Nedi, before Carlo I was alone and after him, I'm alone. It's as if I am not dead or alive. It's as if I've just been crucified. Death is a cross to bear, even for an ordinary person, but everything is a cross for a foreigner: the past, the present, and the future. The cross is heavy, but you must carry it alone. There will be people who want to help you, to carry it for you, like a suitcase, but it's not a suitcase: it is inside, it's in your soul and cuts directly to your heart.' I was only eight years old and, while I tried to understand what she was trying to tell me, like in school when the teacher would read a story to us and then ask us what the author wanted to say, I always stared into space, heart pounding, hands sweaty, and kept thinking that I was too young to reply. I kept imagining Grandma Nedjeljka's cross standing there inside, across her heart. And I couldn't get rid of the image before my eyes: her heart combined with the cross looked like a dartboard; where the vertical and horizontal bars of the cross met was the red spot; only a skilled hand could point the arrow and strike the heart, Grandma's red bullseye.

AH, NEDI, your Granddad Carlo lifted the cross for me as much as he could, he carried it from here to there, up any stairs, he would hold it while waiting for me to come back from wherever I had gone, and he was nearly bent beneath its weight when I came back from Split, the first and second time, but he carried it most of all, I think, when I moved here, when I had carried in my suitcase a wedding dress made of ten metres of satin—there it is, still in the cupboard, but it seems that neither you or Margherita will ever wear it. It's true, your Granddad carried the cross for me as if it were a suitcase, but as I've told you, the cross is not a suitcase, it's not carried in your hand, or on your shoulders or on a cart. It is inside, inside of you, some people call it *life*. But Carlo had his own life-cross, and he couldn't always carry two. Even if he wanted to, he couldn't because the cross that's inside, in the soul that cuts directly to the heart, has no measurable weight. But during his last two years, after he went mute, it was my turn to carry his cross. He didn't let me. Whenever I caressed him, he pushed my hand away, he was embarrassed that I would stroke him like a child. He was ashamed by every tenderness, thinking he earned it as a sick person, not as a husband. He was silent, but in his enormous eyes, eyes that had not diminished, nor framed by wrinkles, all that remained was emptiness. Or fullness from such emptiness. 'But why, Carlo, why?' I would ask, but he'd just look at me. He left without saying a word. I was already seventy-three years old and, even though you always told me I was the youngest Grandma in the world, I was, in fact, already an old woman, with a cross in my soul that carried the weight of souls broken by evil spirits, like your Uncle Luca, left alone, or your Uncle Mario with your cousin Antonio, who never did turn away from neo-Nazi ideas and now is hoping to run for the leadership of the right-wing party, or my brother, whose name will remain unspoken, the name he himself trampled with his malice, or even my mother who never came to see this house that I made my home. But I had no greater cross than your Granddad. When he died, the life-giving organ of life within me died. Maybe it was the cross itself? I don't know. I only know that I wanted to die, too, nothing more. And for that to be my cross. But, they say, God gives people a cross to bear according to the weight they can carry. If so, then I bore everything, carried everything. It seems that in this life everything is no or yes, just like you call me. But how could Carlo die the very morning

I was to go to Split for the third time? Do you remember how much it meant to me that your father and Luca and Mario gave me the airplane ticket? How excited I was by this trip to Split? After nearly thirty years! But to tell you the truth—that's the way it had to be. That way, no other. Your Granddad Carlo died to protect me from that trip. To warn me there was nothing for me in Split, there was no one there who loved me, and the only one left was my brother who had not wanted to see me all these years. Maybe at some point Carlo was sorry that in Bačvice, in the camp, he hadn't killed him, but only broke his finger. Maybe that would have been better for all of us, then Carlo and I would have stayed in Split and I wouldn't have had to learn that moving to a new place is a cross that cuts your heart in two: one part there, the other here. But in life, everything that is bad is for something good. And knowing that, your Granddad didn't wake up that morning. I'm sure your mother said, 'Out of spite' but quietly, so I didn't hear her. No matter how hard your father shook your grandfather to wake him, your Granddad didn't wake up; he knew he didn't need to wake on the day I was supposed to leave for Split. He knew there was no reason for me to go where I was not even a ghost, let alone a woman who had been born and lived there.

YES, NONNA NEDJELJKA, maybe you were no longer even a ghost there, but in our life, in our family, or at least for me, from this side of your biography, you were everything, but not a ghost. At least up until that June 7, 2009, up until my 21st birthday. How beautiful the orange tree in the garden was that day: we all sat around the table, including Margherita's Pietro, and when Margherita said as a joke: 'Now that Neda is 'forever young' she doesn't need a man' and you asked suddenly: 'Which Neda?' and we all started laughing. 'You,' I said as a joke, but everyone else shouted, 'Neda, of course, Neda, not you, you're 86 years old, Neda is 21.' Then you began to scream that you were Neda, that you were twenty-one, that you lived in Split and that Carlo was waiting for you on the Riva. At first, we thought you were joking, and so we also joked along, but soon when you began calling us liars, thieves, and even Fascists, it became apparent that something wasn't right with you. We quickly cleared everything from the table and somehow got you into the house. And just think, in the outdoor refrigerator we forgot the last Split cake you made, especially for me, on the evening before my birthday, not from memory, but from the recipe you had kept since you were young. Several days later your last Split cake had lost all its flavor, and Mamma finally threw it in the garbage. I swear, I think all our hearts were pounding in our temples. We went inside and scattered to our own rooms, and Pietro went home. You went to your room, repeating the whole time you climbed the stairs: 'Fa-scists, Fa-scists!' It was only after all the tests and examinations here and in Trapani when Doctor Rinaldo explained to us that you were suffering from Alzheimer's, that we understood it wasn't hate or spite speaking, as Mamma had said then, but illness, a very concrete, but difficult to understand, illness. Or, easily understandable for your age, for us it was a too-real, too-sick illness. 'Mrs. Nedjeljka Lombardo has a good heart, but her brain is no longer functioning properly, and from now on she will be like this,' the doctor said, 'and worse.' He told us not to leave you alone, and in the evening, we should lock the balcony door in the bedroom. What, so you wouldn't accidentally jump over the railing. At 86 years of age? The doctor said one never knows. But who would lock the balcony door? Papà should have done it, but Mamma spared him, and she told me that I was the one who must lock you in since you were closest to me and I would be the only one you would forgive. There was no greater cross that God—my close family that is—could have placed on my heart! I, your most beloved granddaughter, but more than that, your confidante, your best friend, and namesake, I was the one that had to take your freedom, to kiss you on the forehead each evening while you, with eyes closed as if embarrassed for me, kept repeating: 'Fa-scists, Fa-scists.'

FROM THAT DAY ON, Grandma Nedjeljka had a clinical diagnosis of Alzheimer's and we put the piece of paper with her diagnosis, along with our address and telephone numbers, into the purse she had always carried with her to church or on a walk before her illness. That's what they advised us, then, if she were to slip out without our knowledge and couldn't make her way back home, someone would find the paper and contact us. I had completed my third year of studies that day and I was free the whole summer. I decided not to work anywhere but to 'take care of' Grandma, as everyone said to me. And that 'taking care' wasn't hard. Grandma was calm, like always. She often recalled her past and would tell me about it for hours. No, she couldn't remember what she ate this morning, or where her glasses were.

That was startling to me: she remembered details of her past, but she couldn't recall anything of her day-to-day life. I prompted her to talk, to retell her stories, to recall everything that had marked her past. I already knew it all, but I listened again and again to those stories that were never boring or useless. My mother and Margherita would leave the room when they caught Grandma Nedjeljka repeating something, and Papà felt less and less like listening. Though even he was amazed: how could she remember things from sixty years ago but didn't know whether or not it had rained that morning. It particularly bothered him that if she was told a fact, like how old she was, what her name was, and things like that, she would just repeat: 'I am a young woman, I am twenty-one years old, my name is Neda, my mother is a market peddler, my father is a fisherman, we live in Split.' No one wanted to listen to her stories any longer. But they had to because, thank God, Grandma Nedjeljka lived another five years with Alzheimer's. I finished my studies in Palermo and began working there in a bookstore. I began traveling back and forth to work every day by bus, and my biggest worry was what Grandma would do during that time, whether everything was ok with the woman we had hired to take care of her until Mamma, Papà, and I got back from work. The woman's name was Lea and she was also getting on in years; she was a simple woman from town; the priest had recommended her and we took her; although we knew that her son had been a member of the Mafia, killed by his blood brothers. But Lea said from the very beginning: 'I have no family, I never had a husband, and I got pregnant when I was raped by a scoundrel, but that's how it was, and he was killed. And it's best it turned out that way.' Lea was strange, but in a small town like Castellammare del Golfo there wasn't a big selection of caregivers for old and sick women like Grandma Nedjeljka.

I think Grandma Nedjeljka was mostly calm and obedient for the first three years. She was paranoid the whole time, but it was in the realm of manageable. Whenever she was frightened by something, and every evening when I locked the balcony doors and the door to her bedroom, as the doctor had told us to, she'd usually start shouting: 'Fa-scists, Fa-scists.' In the morning, before I went to Palermo, I unlocked her door, kissed her on the forehead, and left for work. But one day when I entered the room, I didn't see her in the bed. 'Nonna, Nonna Nedjeljka!' I shouted, but I got no answer. Quickly, I looked under the bed and there she was, lying there like a fetus mumbling something unintelligible. 'Grandma Non-Oui,' I called as gently as I could; she looked up at me with fear in her eyes and said: 'Fa-scists, Fa-scists.' 'But Grandma, there are no Fascists here,' I told her, just like I did every other time, 'Come on, come out of there.' I had to drag her out from under the bed myself—some instinct kept me from calling Mamma who was getting ready for work. Lea was to arrive about then. The next morning I found her under the bed again and, once again, I dragged her out and everything was apparently ok, but the third day when I went into the bedroom there, on the floor by the bed, was a small forgotten, childhood tent—one we would sometimes put up in the yard with Grandma, pushing aside the table under the orange tree, and Margherita and I would lay down inside, and Grandma Nedjeljka would sit on the swing and we would each be in our own world without bothering the other. At first, Granddad would walk around the yard, and move the little tent, but later he'd go inside saying: 'All right, enough now, come inside, you shouldn't be sitting out there.' And now she had pulled that little tent from the closet, opened it by the bed and put her pillow inside: that's all the little toy tent could hold. She slept with her head inside, her body curled like a fetus on the floor, with no mattress or blanket. It was as if she had no head, her body lying helplessly as if it had been dumped there. When I saw her all curled up, thin, almost lifeless, I was very upset. Although we tried to take the little tent from her, she simply wouldn't give it up. She cried like a baby and pressed it to her chest. She constantly whispered to me that she was being followed by Fascists and that they were going to come straight into her room through the attic and the roof of the house, and then, she'd say with a feverish sob, it would be terrible, terrible. She wasn't only afraid of Fascists, there were days when she was faint with fear that Ustashi or Italians would come crashing through the windows of the house or that a group of Mafiosi would come through the door and then she'd shout: 'Boom, boom, boom' or she thought Partisans would come up through a crack in the floor, and then Papà, hoping to calm her, would ask as a joke: 'will they be wearing a cap with a five-pointed star or a red scarf?' Sometimes we could hear her crying from the small tent that her brother was coming to take her home to Split. But sometimes she said that Carlo was coming to take her to his world, in heaven, and then she might repeat for hours, as if talking to my Granddad 'But what if God sends me where the Croatians are? You'd be in one place, and I'd be in another. It's not even clear there who's with who.' Why is she talking to him in Croatian, I thought to myself, but it seemed better not to ask.

This was pure paranoia. I asked myself whether everyone with this illness ended like this, or could it be only those with this illness who had had to move somewhere else? That's why I told Papà we should let her keep the tent, but we should spread a rug and mattress so she wouldn't be sleeping directly on the floor. And from that day on, Grandma didn't take her head out of the tent at night. But she also tried to squeeze her body into the one metre space shouting hoarsely: 'Fa-scists, Fa-scists.' The tent became her haven, not only at night, but during the day as well. Lea had to feed her there on the floor, shoving every spoonful of food inside the tent. Mamma already said the time had come for us to find a suitable nursing home for her, and Uncle Luca and Uncle Mario agreed. We saw them rarely, at Christmas or a few days in the summer, but they didn't have a true picture of their mother's illness, and in their phone conversations with Papà, they thought the best decision was for us to place her in a nursing home. Uncle Luca told him to find the best home and he'd pay for it. I heard Papà once say to him: 'Neda won't give her up, she doesn't want us to take her to a home.' I was grateful to him for that. I wanted Grandma Nedjeljka to live to the end of her life in her own home where she had come as a newcomer, and where she had remained as a wife, mother, and grandmother. So she wouldn't have to be a stranger again in a nursing home. She couldn't endure one more move. I tried to make her home even more her own, so she wouldn't also be a ghost in Castellammare del Golfo while she was still alive. In the evenings I would put on movies with the Yugoslav-Italian actress Sylva Coscina that she had liked so much when she was healthy. She liked them now, too, and she could watch the same ones every day, even several times a day. Sometimes Lea also played them for her while we were at work: to give herself some peace, she would play Grandma two or three films on the video player in the living room.

ONE SUNDAY, February 17, 2013, to be precise, a date I will remember for the rest of my life, Mamma, before going to church, asked Grandma Nedjeljka as she usually did, whether she wanted rosemary or basil tea. Grandma was sitting almost motionless at the kitchen table—at my insistence, Papà and I had not abandoned the Sunday morning ritual of bringing her to the kitchen so we could all have breakfast together. Grandma didn't respond. She often didn't answer our questions, but there were moments and days when she repeated every phrase or she'd say something resembling a sentence, a thought. But now she just looked at Mamma with a startled expression and didn't say anything. Then Papà asked her whether she wanted rosemary or basil tea. She didn't answer him either. When I asked her in Croatian, she answered me in Croatian: 'Rosemary.' We gave it to her. That day she would only answer me, briefly, with a word or two at least. She looked quizzically at Mamma and Papà, as if she didn't understand them when they talked to her at breakfast. No one took this as anything other than her feelings towards me, I was the most important person in her life, and she would sometimes not pay attention to anyone else. But the next day, when I went to work and Lea tried to tell her something or ask her something, Grandma just looked at her, listening to her words, but only shaking her head and muttering something 'in that language of hers,' Lea said, 'not in ours.' When I got home, everyone was in a panic, and Mamma called me as I came in the door: 'Neda come here quickly, it's very strange, but your Grandma is either pretending, or she really doesn't understand us anymore.' My heart felt tight. I went in, stroked her hand,

and asked her in Croatian: 'Grandma, Nonna Non-Oui, are you ok? What's bothering you?' 'Well, who are you?' she asked me. 'Nedi,' I said to her loudly, 'don't you remember?' 'You're Nedi?' she said in Croatian, 'And I'm Nedi?' 'Yes, I'm Nedi, Nedjeljka, just like you, don't you remember?' 'Yes, I remember Nedjeljka,' she said to me wearily. 'And do you know Mamma and Papà?' I asked her. 'I don't know,' she said, 'I can't understand them.'

YES, NONNA NEDJELJKA, that is a fact—you had forgotten the Italian language. I don't know myself how it happened, but such events are known in medical literature. Was it over night or gradually? Did your brain at one specific moment shut off its language function or did it happen a little bit each day? Were you only forgetting the language you learned, or could you also be forgetting your mother tongue? 'If it had been gradual, we would have seen it, it would have been obvious,' Papà said, shocked not only by the fact that she had forgotten Italian but also by the fact that he had never learned Croatian so he could continue conversing with you in your mother tongue. Papà doesn't, in fact, have a mother tongue—isn't that absurd? Every person has to have a mother tongue, a real mother tongue that is, not a father tongue, which had become, or thought it had become, the mother tongue as well, due to a particular set of circumstances. But Papà and my uncles didn't have their true mother tongue; they didn't have your language, they only had Italian, their father's language, but is that enough for one person's lifetime? Now, when your illness took away Italian, in effect, it took away your sons, and Antonio, and Margherita, and I was the only one left for you, the only one in the whole family who learned your Croatian language. When you stopped understanding the language you had lived with for more than sixty years, the language of Granddad Carlo and all of us who had been close to you, you lost everyone but me, the only one who could understand you after the short-circuit in your brain evidently erased years and words and an entire language. Mamma didn't believe it at first, and Lea even said to her: 'So how is she watching the Koscina movies? I feel like she understands them.' Yes, you already knew the Koscina movies by heart and you already turned their dialogue into your Croatian, you didn't even think about the words, you knew their meanings by heart. Or, perhaps listening to Koscina, a Croatian in Italy, you understood internally, from the Croatian heart of her Italian roles. I, for one, never believed you lost Italian gradually. I think that's also what Papà believed, but it was easier for him to think that, rather than to acknowledge to himself that he had dedicated so little attention to you in your illness that he hadn't even noticed whether you understood or not. In one way or another, everyone avoided your presence, except on Sundays when they more strongly felt the presence of God because of the ringing of church bells in the city and the view towards St. Mary from your room; they made your presence more visible to them. But as for me, I would have noticed that you were forgetting Italian when they spoke to you or especially when Lea asked you something. You and I only spoke together in Croatian, ever since you taught me as a child and the day you said to me: 'This is the last time I'm going to talk to you in Italian, you know my language well enough now for it to be yours as well.'

And then your Croatian became mine, my Grandma tongue. More and more I feel like you forgot Italian in a single stroke as if inside your brain the fuse for the Italian language burned out, and Boom! Now it's dark, and nothing is visible. Did you truly not remember a single word? Not even *si* or *no*? Did you forget French along with Italian? You hadn't spoken French for years, not since you were young, so it wasn't part of this illness. But did you forget your own name, Non-Oui? It's a good thing that no one here ever called you by the Italian No-Si. It's a good thing that God at least protected you from that, from forgetting your own name.

'She's forgotten the language?' my uncles said in amazement on the telephone. 'How is that possible? How are we going to talk with her now?' 'With an interpreter,' Papà said and looked at me as I went past. 'With an interpreter, with Neda,' he added. All three of them were embarrassed and ashamed that not one of them had ever learned their mother's language, their mother tongue. Lea said she could no longer look after Grandma. 'How can I understand a foreigner?' she said. 'A foreigner,' that's what she said, and in that instant, it became clear to me what Grandma had meant when she said that everything for the foreigner is a cross: past, present, and future. In the end, after everything, the foreigner becomes a foreigner once again; in Grandma Nedjeljka's case, that was literally true, in black and white. She came here as a foreigner, then lived here as someone who adopted this country, or at least she thought it was hers, but in the end, before death, she was turned into a foreigner once again. You are a foreigner most of all where no one understands you and you don't understand anyone. There's a reason that programs to learn the language of one's new fatherland are included in every integration policy. Not only is it desirable, but it's the custom for someone who moves to a new place to learn the language of their new milieu. Grandma Nedjelkja began to learn Italian while she was still living in Split, right after she received that telegram from Granddad saying that they would get married in Sicily. Her Italian might have had a bit of a Slavic accent, but it was the every-day Sicilian dialect, very similar to Granddad Carlo's. Every language has its own gestures, just like people have their own facial expressions in the language they speak; Grandma Nedjeljka took hers from Granddad Carlo's Italian language. Just like I took my Croatian expressions from her Croatian. And now Grandma Nedjeljka—for medical reasons, perhaps her Alzheimer's had reached a new phase, as the doctors said—had forgotten Italian, and though she spoke rarely, she spoke only Croatian. When people addressed her in

Italian, she looked at them with a vacant expression, surprised by the sound of words that she evidently could no longer understand, and which even had no resonance for her at all, as if the language had no echo, not even a shadow of the language.

In the bookstore I searched through all the books on dementia and Alzheimer's but found very little about the loss of language. People wrote that it was important to communicate with such a person as much as possible in the language that remains. But who could communicate with Grandma Nedjeljka except me? In Castellammare del Golfo there were no other Croatians or residents with a Croatian background. During the intervening years, the small town had filled with migrants, mostly from Romania, Albania, and African countries. From the former Yugoslavia, there were virtually no emigrees, or at least we hadn't met any.

At first, I took vacation, an unpaid leave, and I stayed with Grandma Nedjeljka; I took care of her and nursed her as much as I could. When I had used up every option, we begged Lea to come again and at least look after Grandma's physical needs, there was no need to converse with her. She accepted since she hadn't found other work in the meantime. Margherita no longer dropped by Grandma's room, she simply had nothing to say to her, although I could have translated, since I interpreted everything she wanted to tell anyone. Mama, too, spoke minimally to Grandma, but she never skipped muttering 'Out of spite,' although I know it was just from habit, not from impatience with her mother-in-law. Only Papà tried to be a bit more present in her life, speaking to her those few basic words in Croatian—Good morning, How are you? Fine—he had learned, and then Grandma's face would beam with joy and all day she would repeat the greetings 'Dobar den', 'Kako si?' 'Dobro, dobro,' 'Minibus...' Surely Papà's conscience gnawed at him that he had learned only those few words for good morning, how are you, good, and minibus, and not more of Grandma Nedjeljka's language, his mother tongue. Yes, perhaps she was at fault for not teaching her sons Croatian, but when they grew up they could have expressed a desire and a will to learn.

At times I thought it would be good to get in touch with her brother in Split, left alone now with his daughter, so they could speak a little with her, but I didn't know Marina, and throughout my entire life I had only heard bad things about Grandma's brother, Krsto. And if he said anything at all it would just be something nasty, and who needs to hear those words, even if they are in your mother tongue?

MY GRANDMA DIED in her sleep nine months later, on that windy November morning, here in this room, the biggest in the house, which was Grandma and Granddad's, this same room in which my Granddad died in his sleep, the room to which I moved right after her death. Every day I look from the balcony in three directions: to the left the street leads up towards the school, to the right the street leads to St. Mary's, and in front of me stands the house with green curtains which no one has entered for years. On the ground floor, however, there's a bakery that is sometimes open, sometimes closed, sometimes the blinds are up, sometimes they're down. The room where I now spend every day and night was her room, from here I go to work in Palermo, here I sit at the computer, I listen to music, I read, or I lie on her bed, and at night I sometimes wake up without realising where I am. I didn't move the sewing machine which not even Grandma had used for the past ten years, and I, to her great sadness, never learned to sew, but she always said to me: 'Ah, Nedi, your fingers aren't for a needle, but for a book.' Nor did I move the lace doily on the sewing machine that she had brought from Split as part of her small trousseau. I set my laptop on top of the lace doily, and from time to time I glance at that strange combination of eras, and it isn't clear to me whether my Grandma understood my era—she lived a long time, a full 91 years—nor whether I understood hers. In the drawer of the nightstand there is still the ticket for Split that Papà and my uncles bought for her in 1996, but that morning before the flight Granddad Carlo died and she never traveled there again. In addition to the ticket there is still her small, now-dilapidated

Serbo-Croatian-Italian dictionary and 'Free Dalmatia' the first Split edition no. 28 from 1943. There were a few photographs, of her father and her mother, but none of her brother. Nor were there any of Charlotte. In the dictionary, however, there was a photo of Grandma in her youth and on the back in faded letters was written 'From Charlotte'. Charlotte must have taken the picture with her journalist's camera. But why hadn't they taken their picture together or with someone else? Or perhaps they had taken such pictures, but she didn't bring them with her. Maybe she thought she would never forget the faces of those closest to her, but even the faces of those nearest to us are forgotten in the course of time, no matter how much we want to hold them in our memory; if you don't see people at least occasionally, they slowly fade and one day you realize you no longer remember what Charlotte looked like, or young Marcel, or your French teacher, or Yulia or Krunoslav...and when you realize that you no longer remember what your mother looked like, you simply get the shivers, and you fear that you will forget everything that remains, the house in which you were born, the entrance to the house, the narrow Split streets, and even the sea, yes, even the sea because every sea has its own colour, its own sound, its own quiet. When I think about her words, I pull out from under the bed the child's tent in which Grandma Nedjeljka's head slept until her death, while her body lay on the mattress on the floor. I unfold the sides, set it on the floor, put a pillow inside. I pull the cover from the bed and lie down the way Grandma did. In my dream, I see Grandma's hands and feet, but not her head hidden in the tent. Maybe we should have put the tent in her coffin. But we would have had to place it on top of her body but that didn't seem right to cover her completely. And we couldn't buy a wider coffin because we had decided to bury her in the garden under the orange tree. Alone, in her own cemetery. That's what she wanted and told us when she was still healthy and aware: 'Don't bury me in the cemetery! I don't think I want to be among strangers again when I'm dead. Bury me wherever you want, but not with other dead people.' She didn't want us to bury her with Granddad Carlo either. 'Carlo and I no longer understand one another, he's silent, I talk,' she said. During the last months, they wouldn't have understood one another's language either. Mamma thought we should bury her in Split, that is, we could send her by air and her brother and niece could bury her, but she changed her mind, thank God, when she heard that international burials like that cost as much as three times Papà's salary. And so, Mamma somehow persuaded us to bury her in the garden under the orange tree. To the horror of the neighbours and the sanitation inspectors. I paid the fine from my pay, along with the bribe to the inspector. I also signed a form saying that once a week we would use a special substance to disinfect the grave. And that we would never destroy the garden or put up a lower fence around the house, which would upset passersby and the neighbours who would see the grave. I signed all sorts of things, whatever was put in front of me. On the gravestone we wrote: Nedjeljka Lombardo, nee Jagnjić, Split 1923—Castellammare del Golfo 2014. We didn't write Spalato but Split, in her and my Croatian language. And below, in small letters I carved with a gardening knife: NON-OUI.

IN 1996, at the age of seventy-three, Grandma Nedjeljka got her airplane ticket Trapani-Trieste-Split; she often held it, examined it, reread it, and I think she felt like it was a ticket to some other world, not an ordinary airline ticket for a trip, and when she was supposed to set off that morning, my Granddad didn't wake up, 'Out of spite' my mother later said, but quietly, so my Grandma wouldn't hear; Margherita thought Granddad Carlo was pretending, making a joke so Grandma would be afraid she'd miss her flight; my father shook him by the shoulder and called to him 'Papà, Papà' but my Granddad really did not wake up, and my Grandma stayed home and never again traveled to Split.

Nearly twenty years later I went, eight months after my Grandma's death. Just like that, I bought a ticket on the Internet: Trapani-Trieste-Split-Trapani, because I felt empty and aimless in my life. I thought that it was only in Grandma Nedjeljka's birthplace that I could find her again, and along with her, my own joy in life, some meaning for my 27 years of life, some justification for my life, because those eight months without her seemed to be the worst months of my life. Although she had been sick for a long time and incapable of doing anything, my awareness that she only understood me, me and no one else, that I was her only connection to the world around her, and that her actual physical presence in the house meant so much to me and I simply couldn't get used to the fact that she was no longer there. Why hadn't I visited Split earlier and why in some way did I wait for her to die first and then go to the place she left to go to Granddad's home? It wasn't clear to me. In our home one simply didn't ask about traveling to Split. After 1996, when

Grandma Nedjeljka did not travel to Split with the ticket that had already been purchased, it didn't occur to anyone to buy her another, and it didn't occur to her either. With Granddad Carlo's death, Split died for her as well. At least, as a real, physical, destination. I once asked Papà why we never made it possible for her to travel to Split again, he answered: 'Because your Grandma wasn't like that. As if she'd travel after your Granddad's death! And what would she say to her brother if she turned up at his place in Split? "Carlo died, so here I am." Ah, she wouldn't give her brother that pleasure. And besides, she wasn't a widow like the ones I often drive on the bus to Scopello or Erice. To tell you the truth, I sometimes have the impression that there are some women, and men, too, who wait for their spouses to die, the sooner the better, so they can travel the world alone. Either alone, with new partners, or simply in the company of other people. Most of the time they're on trips organized through agencies or I don't know, some sort of organizations for retirees, chess players, former teachers. You name it!' And Papà, because of the opinions he had formed as a driver, had allowed Split to become an impossible goal for Grandma. But who knew Grandma Nedjeljka the best? Who spoke most often with her both in this world and the next? Who didn't get bored when she told and retold her stories? Only me, that's a fact. I was the only one who had learned her language. And I was, therefore, the one who felt most compelled to go to Split, and that was eight months after we buried her under the orange tree in the garden. I did all the formalities: on Facebook I found Marina, Grandma Nedjeljka's niece, but she didn't accept me, just sent a message: 'It's a good thing you got in touch, because my father has wanted to know something for a long time: after your Grandma died, did you find a small bone hidden somewhere, one of her father's bones, from when they dug him up in Sustipan and they had to bury him again in the new cemetery?' Apparently, after his sister's death, that's all her father thought about, about where this bone was, the last remains of his father, and, even though when she was in Split Grandma had denied knowing anything about it, he was certain she had it. But we didn't find anything like that among her things. There was nothing like that in any of the cupboards, or drawers in her room, or in the whole house. I told Mamma, and she said that if Grandma did have that bone from her father, she would have hidden it in the pocket of the blazer we buried her in. 'Her brother can now just come and dig her up if he wants to find it!' That's what she said, but I, of course, didn't write that to my aunt or whatever she was to me. 'We haven't found anything like that,' I wrote to her, and, as politely as possible, I asked her a few questions—how they were, whether her father was in good health, whether she would come visit us in Castellammare del Golfo, alone or with friends, perhaps with her co-workers, I didn't mention anything about a partner, since I suspected that she had remained unmarried, and must be fifty years old, but she didn't answer me. But how happy I was that she had at least written me that first message. Blood doesn't have to be water, at least that's what I thought, although Grandma Nedjeljka, whenever she spoke about her brother, always said to me: 'Ah, Nedi, blood isn't water, but water is blood.' I have to admit I'm not even sure today what she was trying to tell me.

In the end, I wrote to Marina that I was coming to Split, and I set off. My mother's departing words to me were: 'Look around and find someone, so your trip isn't just for spite, at least there you won't have a problem with your name.' My father asked me whether I was going to visit Uncle Mario since I was traveling through Trieste. 'No, I don't have time,' I told him, although, the truth was that after Grandma Nedjeljka's death, my father and my uncles had become estranged, and through them, so did we, the cousins. Especially with Uncle Mario's family, but that had happened years ago, when he came to tell us that my cousin Antonio had become a neo-Nazi and he wanted us to take him in during the holidays and I cried and shouted that I didn't want him to come. Although I was a child, Uncle Mario apparently took offence and Antonio didn't visit us until Granddad Carlo died. He, a confirmed right-winger, simply didn't show up for Grandma's burial. Nor did we go to Trieste any longer, and now, when I had to fly from Trieste to Split, even though it would have been normal for me to at least call them, I could find no reason to; Grandma Nedjeljka was dead and with her death all the reasons for closeness with the wider family had gone to the devil. My father told me just to bring him back a shell from Split, so he could hear the sea more clearly. In the meantime, Margherita had moved in completely with Pietro, and was now pregnant, but unhappy. Pietro spent more time with the children in the rented apartment where their mother had moved, than with her, now in the third month of her pregnancy with their first child. 'What's the baby's name?' I asked her before I left. 'Will you name him in honour of Granddad?' 'When you have a child, you can go and name him Carlo,' she said to me. 'I won't name mine that.' Whether because of Grandma Nedjeljka's recent death, or because I was leaving, we were all tense and nervous. I boarded the bus for Trapani and from there took a taxi to the airport.

NONNA NEDJELJKA, my Grandma Non-Oui, I am flying to your city. Next to me on the plane is an older man; he's been dozing the whole time, and his head occasionally hits the window. Seated in front of me is a young, unattractive couple watching a film on a white Apple laptop. The guy—brown beard, big head, and thick brown hair with short bangs. The woman— hair slicked back in a ponytail, short-sleeved t-shirt with 'Hard Rock' written across the back. And I think to myself—did she put it on backwards or are some shirts designed like that? And I laugh to myself: maybe she put it on backwards to keep herself from being afraid of the flight? They love each other in a weary way, like an old couple, or maybe a new one, still not needing closeness. The Apple glows a fluorescent white. On my left, two men. They are speaking Croatian, one of them says he's going to Split to sell his house where a whole family from Bosnia found safety during the war and stayed. 'Yeah, what's a house to you in Split? In Mestre you live in a one-room apartment, while there you have a house, at least this way you'll be able to treat yourself more.' 'But it's no life living alone,' said the man with the house. 'You have to have people around you who are close: friends, relatives.' The other man was silent. After a while he says, 'Yeah, otherwise you become a loner.' 'And how,' says the man with the house. 'And how,' repeats his friend.

No one was waiting for me in Split. The day before I left, I wrote to Marina on Facebook to tell her I was coming, and what time I would arrive, but they didn't need to feel any obligation towards me, I would make my own way. But I would like to see her father and become acquainted with her. I added that on the Internet I had found a little apartment, and I would be spending two weeks there, and that was all. 'Blood isn't water, but water is blood' isn't that what you said to me? Even today I wonder what you wanted to tell me. Still, somewhere in the bottom of my heart I had hoped at the airport I'd find Marina, your niece through your brother, now a grown woman already. But there was no one. I got on bus 37 and reached the city. It wasn't difficult finding the little street where the apartment was located, but I had to follow the app on my telephone. In front of the entrance, I had to wait a bit for the owner of the apartment to give me the key. My Croatian surprised her. She said to me: 'Ah, if only all the tourists knew Croatian like that! It's just *dobar dan* and *hvala*; All they learn is *good morning* and *thank you* and, even that with mistakes and they think they're very clever.' Evidently the woman had a hard time with the tourists in Split. But I was in your city for the first time, and I had no time for anger. I opened the blinds and windows in the small apartment, unpacked, and went out. I devoured the city where I fell in love with each new step along its narrow streets. Still, my thoughts led me to the Old Town, to your old house where your 85-year-old brother and his 51-year-old unmarried daughter now lived. If the genes are passed down, it's possible that I'll live to such an old age like you did, and now your brother, still, God protect me from being struck by dementia. But if the family fate follows us, that means both Marina and I will either remain old maids, unmarried, or maybe I'll get married at an old age like your brother. I'm well along that path, aren't I, Grandma Non-Oui?

It wasn't difficult finding your house; with a smart phone in hand everything is easier, except for one's inner life. I stood ten minutes in front of the house, looking at it, trembling with excitement. I saw the stairs you told me about that led up to your floor, after your aunt had left the house. And I remembered your father's fishing boots that your aunt tripped over and miscarried for the second time. It now looked like no one was living upstairs, although the upper windows and shutters were wide open, but on the lower window, right by the entry door, only the shutters were open. I rang the bell. Marina immediately opened the door. It was obviously her, even though I had never seen her before. She looked quizzically at me, but it was soon clear to her who I was, and to me that she had seen my message on Facebook. 'Neda? Is that you?' I went inside and from the hallway I saw your brother in a wheelchair. 'Papa, your sister Nedjeljka's granddaughter is here,' she said to him loudly, word by word, as if to a thick-headed child. 'The bone...' he muttered without offering me his hand, without raising his head. 'I beg your pardon?' I asked, not understanding his first word, 'the bone.' 'Don't pay any attention to him,' Marina whispered to me, 'he doesn't recognize anyone anymore, he only mutters something about the bone that your Grandma supposedly took from their father when they reburied him. At least that's what he said to me a while ago, when he was still healthy.' It was apparent that my great-uncle Krsto, if I can call him that, was in no condition to have any conversation, any meeting with me. 'I couldn't leave him alone to come to the airport,' Marina said as she served me juice and wafer cookies. And then we fell silent, but after a few minutes I asked whether I could go upstairs to the floor where Grandma Nedjeljka had lived. 'Go up, but there isn't anything there now. I threw everything away. Workmen whitewashed the apartment three days ago. I've put in a new parquet floor and the bathroom is new. I'll rent it out to tourists, I've been left without work at the school; I wasn't cut out for teaching history, and Papa's illness is expensive, with just a single pension you can't make it through the month.' So that's how it is, Nonna, Marina threw everything out, into the trash! She didn't preserve the smallest scrap of your past. She, who had apparently been a history teacher. Or maybe that's why? The furnishings on the ground floor were old, but not that old, it looked like new furniture had been bought in the eighties. 'What will you do in Split? Have you come on holiday? It's already full on Bačvice!' Marina said. Your brother slept the whole time in the wheelchair. He didn't lift his head even once, and I'm not sure he could. I got up, there was nothing for me to do with these people in this house. Nonna, you were no longer even a ghost or someone who had once lived there. I'm sorry I have to tell you this, but I felt you had died twice: first, the true, physical death in Castellammare del Golfo, and then as a person, a spirit, in Split.

I walked every day through the town and every day I worked out a path that took me by your house. I don't know why: revenge, memorializing, eternalizing? Everything was in your honour. But Split was full of tourists; in some of the narrow streets we literally had to elbow our way past one another. There was noise down below the apartment day and night. Languages, sounds, groups with tour leaders, morning cleaners and garbage collectors, nighttime merry making. Sounds that sweeten the night like the jazz that rolled down towards the square flowing like water, and sounds that ripped through the night, like the man shouting, waking me the second night. Waves of people with their high, penetrating voices struck at my loneliness and unwittingly reminded me of yours when you moved to Castellammare. One night in my sleep I was driven crazy by a man and woman quarrelling in English. I thought to myself, people argue even more when they're traveling. But they usually travel to make peace. I woke up, fell back asleep, then woke again. I went early to the beach. The water was shallow and there were clusters of children, grandfathers, grandmothers, young people, and babies. Everyone who wasn't going to work or to school was already on Bačvice. The young people in the shallows were playing a ball game, and it was even hard to enter the water where, with their loud cries, curses, and frenetic motion they had taken over the sea as if they owned it. There was a large billboard on the beach advertising Ožujsko beer and Picigin. That's when I remembered that Picigin was the Split ballgame, a game that existed even when you were little. So, this was Bačvice where your brother Krsto sang Dalmatian songs to the Italian soldiers? Yes, I also found the Hotel Park, the former Italian headquarters, imagine that! And this is where Granddad Carlo broke his finger? But I hadn't thought about his finger at all when I was there! How had that slipped my mind? Your brother's hands were under a blue blanket, maybe that's why. But Granddad Carlo had broken that finger in a way that lasted his whole life, right?

On the third day, I got on the rickety, yellow No. 12 bus and went to the Bene beach below Marjan. *Marjane, Marjane...* Was there anyone left who still knew that song? In Split it feels as if the Partisan past has been swept away forever without a trace. But it's more than that: I read in 'Free Dalmatia' that just a day ago, a huge swastika was etched on the stadium pitch at the Croatia—Italy soccer match. 10 metres long by 10 metres wide!

It gave me the goosebumps: did it have to be Italy and Croatia playing that day? 'Out of spite' Mamma would say. Nonna, it's a good thing that you and Nonno are no longer alive. Fascism is returning to Europe. Perhaps it never disappeared. Still, it wasn't fair—how can I put this—that until your death the word you said to us most often was 'Fascists.'

But many other things happened here, that's very clear to me now. In the nineties more happened than even during the time of the Italian, and later, German occupations, that is, during your time. No, not because of the casualties, but because of the era. Wasn't the Second World War to be a lesson for all nations in the world not to fight any longer? No, Nonna Nedjeljka. At least not here, especially during the nineties and beyond. As you know, the greatest crimes since the Holocaust took place in your Yugoslavia. Your brother's wife experienced it herself, though she only experienced one percent of everything that could have happened to her. She was a Serb in Split. Once the shooting began in Vukovar between Serbs and Croats, she was suddenly no longer a good neighbor or a good saleswoman in the 'Jadran textiles' store or a good Split wife, or a good Split mother, everyone looked at her askance, as if she had killed someone. In some way, it's a good thing that she got cancer right at the start of the war. That is, she discovered then that she was in an advanced stage. She died quickly, without pain. Both physically and mentally. But Marina, frightened by the *Serb* half inside her, wondered whether she should beg us to bring her to Castellammare—and you know yourself we would have taken her—or whether she should remain in Split. She decided to remain in Split; out of shame, she didn't ask us, you, that is, the mortal enemy of her father, to shelter her as long as things went on in Yugoslavia. Things that you did not witness, thank God. But your brother and Marina did. She told me about it herself when she came looking for me on my fourth day in Split and brought me half a Split cake, 'In Split you must try our

197

special Split cake,' she said laughing as if she didn't feel right coming to find me only after I stopped going to their place. I told her that you made the best Split cake. Once again, blood is not water. She told me she had left her father bathed and fed, with clean underwear and a sliced banana sitting in front of the television to watch soccer and she came to take me on an outing to see something outside of Split. 'I'll take you to Vrlika,' she said. I hadn't heard of that small, tranquil town beneath the Dinaric Alps; you had never mentioned it to me. Along the way, she pointed out to me the place where there had earlier been an artificial lake, created in the '60s when the leaders, in an agreement with the villagers, flooded six or seven villages and an entire Serbian Orthodox monastery. Maybe you knew about something like that? On television someone once said that when the lake dried up, he saw the monastery: collapsed, moldy, green. 'What about God?' Marina said. 'What do you think, Neda, can God also turn moldy?' 'It depends on the person,' I said with teeth clenched. 'No, not on the person, it depends on the church, or more specifically on the priest who blesses the army,' she said. We circled Vrlika: gorgeous land-scapes, on the right-side fertile fields, and on the left a cliff that the government had planted with evergreens. We stopped by the stone bridge, down below in the river Cetina the stones lay like hippos in the water. Marina pointed out to me an early Christian church—preserved ruins, a bell tower, and around it— Orthodox graves with inscriptions in Cyrillic belonging to the villagers from the nearby villages inhabited predominantly by Serbs. 'In the nineties, the houses here were torched,' she said. 'First the Serbs torched the Croatian ones, and then, for revenge, the Croatians torched the Serbs. Today they live apart, Serbs in Serbian neighbourhoods, Croatians in Croatian neighbour-hoods.' They forgave each other, but they forgot nothing about what they had done. I learned that the first Croatian opera, 'Ero the Joker' was written in Vrlika in 1935 by Jakov Gotovac, with a libretto by Milan Begović, and it may have been translated into Italian as well. We stood in the amphitheatre where it is performed every year and then Marina took a book from her bag and gave it to me: 'You can't buy it anymore, it's sold out, but if you want to know something about the dark side of Split, read it.' The book was called *Poems from Lora* by Boris Dežulović. 'Boris Dežulović!' I cried out. 'I read him in *Free Dalmatia* on the Internet.' 'You won't be able to read him there anymore. He submitted his resignation yesterday,' she said and added 'Croatia is much more complicated than you can imagine.' Nonna Nedjeljka, it seems that that is the truth.

I ASKED HER ABOUT CHARLOTTE, and Marcel, and Yuri, about all the people you had told me about, people I felt were also close to me although I had never met them. She didn't know them. Charlotte was surely no longer alive, and maybe Marcel wasn't either. She said she had never heard of a woman by the name of Charlotte in Split. But not long ago someone mentioned that a photographer from France had visited Split, someone with a French name and a Croatian last name. But she didn't remember either of the names. Maybe that was Marcel? From what you told me, I didn't know exactly where they had lived, somewhere near the church 'Our Lady of Health' in Dobri, but I couldn't point out the exact place to her. She hadn't heard anything about the Russians who had once lived there either. Her father, while he was still healthy, had never mentioned them to her. 'His whole life he was either angry and shouting, or silent,' she said and then bit her lip. 'But for the last three years he just mumbles. He doesn't shout and he's not silent.'

In the apartment that evening I read Dežulović's *The Poems from Lora*. I had diarrhea that night. I dreamt about a child who couldn't dry his wet leg because Hitler himself was stalking him. He finally manages to dry his leg, but his skin is like potato peel, and he runs away. In my dream, I was relieved that the child escaped, and I woke up. And in that instant, I understood that people rarely escaped the camp here, near Split, in Lora where Croatian patriots locked up Serbian prisoners of war, civilians who looked suspicious to someone, and any person who was not aware of what it meant to be a Croat. Each and every poem was a confession from the sick mind of the criminals. A reverse perspective on evil. A text for the archive, not just for the bookshelf. Such books could, and perhaps were, written about Knin, and Srebrenica, about Vukovar, and Sarajevo, and about many other places in the former, wider fatherland that belonged to Grandma Nedjeljka. Each war, it seems, has two perspectives.

The second week of my stay in Split I tried to watch more Croatian television to see what was happening in the country. The lead stories were all about the migrant crisis, about how that summer was hellish in the region, not just because of the temperature but also because of the refugees from Syria and other countries who were attempting to get to Western Europe along the Western Balkan route. They were about how the number of refugees was greater than we have back home in Italy, but how, fortunately, in Croatia one didn't sense it. About how at the borders between Greece and Macedonia, Macedonia and Serbia, and Serbia and Hungary there was chaos, and it was only a matter of time before the wave of refugees would be redirected towards Croatia and Slovenia. One commentator stated that Europe was becoming more and more right-wing, and that reminded me of my cousin Antonio, who had already become one of leaders in right-wing politics in Italy.

I went to the movie theatre and film library 'Zlatna vrata' several times. The first time I asked the people working there to put on a USB flash drive the most important Croatian films from the Second World War, which, according to Marina were the series about Split, *Velo misto*, and *Malo misto*. I watched them on my tablet while I sat on a bench on the Riva, headphones on, and I thought to myself the whole time: 'Ah, if only Grandma

Nedjeljka could see these!' They were films about her era, about the Split she knew firsthand, but also about Granddad Carlo's era. In the film library, I saw they were playing an adult animated film with the curious title 'Rocks in my pockets,' a Latvian-American co-production. The film is about madness, about women, about the urge to suicide. It was so good, and I felt it related to me so much. I noticed that all the seats in the hall were named for directors or actors. I laughed when I realized that I had been sitting the whole time in the lap of Almodóvar. Of course, I also went to the movie theatre 'Karaman' where Grandma Nedjeljka had gone with her girlfriends, and I suspect it hasn't changed much since then. A brand-new Croatian film with the title *You Carry Me* exhausted me and filled me with sadness.

My second-to-last day I went to see the sculptures of Ivan Meštrović—Grandma Nedjeljka's Meštrović—about whom there's a large volume in Italian in the bookstore in Palermo, but it's so expensive we haven't been able to sell it for two years. From this book, I had become acquainted with all his statues, but in real life, they were more beautiful, brighter. Still, I kept asking myself: what possessed him—the worm of ego, which not even the purest souls can avoid, or was it the command of an angel, an archangel—to paint himself on the dome of the chapel in which he and his family were buried? Was it so he could see himself from a higher, more divine perspective? In the garden in front of the gallery a turtle lazily nibbled a white flower and green grass. The sculptures—large, smooth, superhuman —watched it attentively. At the entry desk I took a photocopy of Augustine Rodin's 1915 letter to Meštrović in which he tells him that as soon as he can, he'll send the sculptor 'Meditation—Internal Voice', which now stands right beside Meštrović's 'Psyche'. I bought the 2016 calendar which portrayed his sculptures. In the bookstore beside his monument to Marulić, I looked for books by Dubravka Ugrešić, but they didn't have a single one. I wondered aloud how this was possible, but the saleswoman just shrugged her shoulders. 'Even in the bookstore where I work in Palermo we have four of Ugrešić's books,' I said to her, 'in Italian.' *The Ministry of Pain,* and *The Culture of Lies*, and *Baba Yaga laid an egg* and *The Museum of Unconditional Surrender;* I listed them trying to translate the titles correctly into Croatian. The saleswoman said nothing, just looked through me, as if gazing through the shop window. In my agitation, I headed to the statue of Gregory of Nin, I touched his huge toe for good luck, but at that instant I couldn't think of a single thing to wish for.

As I was leaving, I went by Marina's house once more. I could no longer call it 'Grandma Nedjeljka's house.' There, my Grandma was neither a ghost nor a person who had, in another time, lived at the same address. I found her brother, Great-Uncle Krsto, on the first-floor dozing in his wheelchair, just as before. This time he wasn't covered with a blanket. And I saw the little finger on his left hand, hanging like a dried-up little bone. He was already a ghost with one foot in the grave. Marina gave me a small red bag as a gift: inside she had placed a CD by Oliver Dragojević. 'This is the most famous Croatian singer,' she told me. 'Maybe your father will like it. He was born in 1947, the year your Grandma left Split.' It was then I recalled Papà's request to bring him a shell from Split. I went into the first souvenir shop and bought the biggest and loudest.

NONNA NEDJELJKA, I dreamt of you last night: you are sitting beside this table in the garden, and I just walk around you saying to myself: 'Oh, Grandma Non-Oui, Oh, Grandma Non-Oui,' and you answer: 'Ah, Nedi, something is bothering you, something isn't right.' Then we both sit and weep. And you tell me that if you had a brother among the living, you would only do good to him, if only he were alive. But in reality, your brother is alive, there, in Split, and you are dead. Who will do something good for whom? In the end, apparently only Margherita, since she named her son Cristiano. Not after your brother, but after a famous Portuguese soccer player who was Pietro's favourite. But still.

I woke and around noon I got a message on Facebook: Marina wrote me that her father had died. Three days ago. They had already buried him. She was alone at the burial, along with the priest. Great-Uncle Krsto had no friends or relatives in Split. She called several of her former colleagues from the school where she had taught history; not a single one came. She was only telling us now because she didn't want any of us to consider going on such a journey. Plus, she says, she's not sure her father would have given permission for anyone from your side of the family to come to his burial. As if he would have known if anyone had been there! When I told Mamma and Papà, Papà said that either way none of us would have gone. I was sorry about that somehow. For Marina, who was now entirely alone in the house. But soon tourists will begin to arrive, and she will hear human voices on the upper floor. And she will clean up the first floor, throw away all her father's things, just as she had done with her mother's, and yours, too, of course. Maybe she'll also rent rooms to tourists on the first floor, with a shared bath and kitchen. Or maybe she'll sell the house, as more and more of the people living in towns along the coast do, even here in Castellammare del Golfo, and she'll move to Vrlika, to one of the abandoned apartments at the edge of town. And what will she do in the years to come? Will she look for work? Find a husband? Is it too late to begin a new life? She will certainly continue to read. Maybe she'll become a volunteer in a humanitarian organization providing joint summer vacations for Croatian and Serbian children who live there. Or she could even become an activist for human rights. And why not even a volunteer in the refugee camps? Older women end up there too, not just young people. But there aren't any refugee camps there now. Europe got rid of the refugee crisis by relocating it to Turkey.

I see her posts on Facebook with articles and photographs of protests across Croatia. Two thousand people gathered on the square in Zagreb shouting, 'Resign, resign, resign,' and 'We do not want a sympathizer of the Ustashi Independent State of Croatia as minister of culture.' There was even a petition signed by a large number of international artists and intellectuals opposed to the Croatian minister of culture, Zlatko Hasanbegović. There among the names were our Dario Fo and Antonio Negri. There was also the name of someone named Marcel, a photographer in Paris. Marcel? Marcel with a Croatian last name? My heart was pounding. That had to be that Marcel, Charlotte's, and Grandma Nedjeljka's. He would now be more than 70 years old! So, he had become a well-known photographer and had even signed the petition against the Croatian minister of Culture. I search to see what the Minister of Culture has done to turn everyone against him. At work I have so many obligations as head of the literature division that I no longer have time to read *Free Dalmatia*, plus I had gotten out of the habit ever since last year when Boris Dežulovič stopped writing his column. I see that the Minister of Culture is a real 'case'. He doesn't recognize the tragedy of the Jasenovac camp where Grandma's French teacher, Charlotte's husband, perished. He is pro-Ustashi and longs for that Independent State of Croatia in which Grandma Nedjeljka lived. On the anniversary of that party's founding, 75 years later, people from cultural sectors gathered to demand his resignation and to proclaim that, in Croatia, right-wing policies were gaining strength among the ruling elite, especially, through the Minister of Culture. That is why there were five thousand signatures belonging to people from cultural sectors within Croatia and outside it. How come there was nothing about this in the Italian papers? The Serbian premier went to Croatia and in his speech he said that 75 years ago a monstrous state, the Independent State of Croatia, was created, a criminal state which surpassed all the Nazi dreams for the eradication of other races.

'Did anything happen in Split?' I couldn't help asking Marina. 'Yes, of course,' she answered me, 'A while ago, HDS —The Croatian Defensive Forces—they're neo-Nazis, you know, announced that, in Split, there would be a joint march with the Society of the Urban Right in support of the Minister of Culture.'

And the greatest stupidity of all? A woman had the idea to propose a ban on the reading of certain authors in the high schools, authors such as Dubravka Ugrešić, Slavenka Drakulić, and several other Croatian writers, as well as foreign authors like Murakami andMarguerite Duras. Apparently, these books contain pornography harmful to young people. When I read that, an idea immediately came to me: in the bookstore in Palermo, I would put up an exhibit: 'Forbidden Authors in Croatia', even though ordinary people hadn't even heard of Croatia. But readers are not ordinary people, are they? As a bookseller, I expect more from them. And in fact, the Italian editions we had by those forbidden authors in Croatia, sold more in those three days than any other books. I thought to myself: this is my legacy from Grandma Nedjeljka. Her remarkably beautiful and wondrous, miraculous Croatia. *Croatia, Full of Life*—that's the advertisement for Croatia that's broadcast on Italian television. A land full of life, one way or another. A life that forgets the dead who made that life possible for it, and a life that celebrates the dead that buried her while she was still living.

BUT YOU, NONNA NEDJELJKA, count yourself lucky that you are not alive and that you are no longer a ghost in Split. Especially since they're raising fascist monuments and destroying Partisan ones. As Marina wrote me in her last message: in today's Croatia, no one wants to recall the time of the Second World War when the Croats, Serbs, and Bosnians were one and fought together against their joint enemy, against Nazi Germany and the fascist Italian army, and against those domestic traitors: the Ustashi and the Chetniks. And the anti-fascism of that time is only good for the Constitution, but the Constitution has long since been turned into a piece of paper no one respects. The Minister of Culture even announced: 'anti-fascism is an empty phrase.' An empty phrase? Between birth and death, life is everything but an empty phrase. But anti-fascism is life for some, death for others.

Split and Castellammare del Golfo intersect and pound into my heart like a wedge: both were your life and your death. I feel Split pulling me, calling me, but Castellammare holds me and does not loose me from its grasp. Beautiful places that will not save the world, or any of us.

The fact that the government of Croatia fell on 16 June is news not only of the day, but of the year. 'I thank you Orešković. That was your best move during your term,' someone wrote. 'Open Twitter,' Marina wrote to me. 'I don't have it,' I answered. So, she copied the most interesting posts and sent them to me. And what did I see?! Twitter was flooded with bare-breasted Croatian women. Just imagine, there had been a movement as part of the anti-government protests: 'Breasts in support of the fall of the government;' on the day the government fell, every woman would bare her breasts and post a photograph on Twitter. Because of this initiative, people on Twitter could barely wait for the government to fall. 'Well, Marina, did you photograph yourself?' I asked. She sent me dozens of people laughing, laughing like crazy, clutching their stomachs, and below she wrote: 'I celebrated the fall of the government a different way, I put on a coat, winter boots, cap, shawl, and mittens and that's how I went out to the Riva. In 35-degree heat!'

Just like Grandma Nedjeljka, I wanted to write back, but I changed my mind. I'll save that memory for myself. Grandma wore the red, felt beret with a small silk tassel, a gift from Charlotte, on the Riva in Split on September 8, 1943, the day Italy capitulated and in the days that followed; it was still on her head when she wiped Granddad Carlo's bloody ear and fell in love with his enormous eyes. And there was Grandma on the Riva in Split in her red beret on 26 October 1945, the first anniversary of the liberation of the city. And then in Sustipan with Carlo, Krsto, and her mother—happy in Split for the last time. A life-cross.

But life is always *Yes*. Death is always *No*. It was just the other way around, Nonna, in your name, Grandma Non-Oui. First you were *no*, then you were *yes*.

LIDIJA DIMKOVSKA (b. 1971, Skopje, North Macedonia) is a poet, writer, and translator from Romanian and Slovenian into Macedonian, living in Slovenia. She has published seven books of poetry, four novels, an American diary, a collection of short stories, and has edited four anthologies. Her books have received numerous awards, among them the Macedonian awards for best prose book of the year (twice) most recently in 2024 for her novel *Personal Identification Number*. In 2024 she was also named Author of the Year at the Skopje Book Fair. She has also been awarded best poetry book of the year, the European Union Prize for Literature, the German Hubert Burda Prize, the Slovenian 'Glass of Immortality' etc. Her books have been translated in fifteen languages. In English translation she has published her novel *A Spare Life* (Two Lines Press, 2016, longlisted for the 2017 Best Translated Book Award) and her poetry collections *What is it Like?* (Wrecking Ball Press, 2022), *pH Neutral History* (Copper Canyon Press, 2012, shortlisted for the 2013 Best Translated Book Award), and *Do Not Awaken Them With Hammers* (Ugly Duckling Presse, 2006).

Excerpts from her novels, poems, essays, interviews and reviews about her books appeared in, among others: Times Literary Supplement, American poetry Review (the cover page and a special supplement), World Literature Today, Frankfurter Allgemeine Zeitung, The Rumpus, Tin House, the Paris Review, the Literary Hub, Foreword, The White Review, Asymptote, Publishers Weekly, BBC World Service, Words Without Borders, Columbia Journal, Los Angeles Review, Boston Review, Poetry International, Plume, etc.

CHRISTINA E. KRAMER is a professor emerita of Slavic languages and linguistics at the University of Toronto. Throughout her career, she has combined her love for languages, linguistics, and literature. She is the author of many articles on Balkan linguistics and a Macedonian grammar. Her translations from Macedonian have been awarded prizes, including support from the National Endowment for the Arts, Pen Translates, UK, Lois Roth Honorary Mention, and long-listed for Best Translation of the Year (USA). Her translations have also appeared in numerous journals, including *Asymptote, Brooklyn Rail, Chicago Review, Modern Literature, M-Dash, The Punch Magazine, Tin House, Two Lines, Words without Borders, World Literature Today*. A complete list of these works and links to many online excerpts and short translations can be accessed at

www.christinakramertranslator.ca.